MAGGIE MILLER

PIGEON FORGE CHRISTMAS

A MOUNTAIN HOME CHRISTMAS

A MOUNTAIN HOME CHRISTMAS
Copyright © 2024 Maggie Miller

Still grieving the loss of her husband, Maddie retreats to the peaceful isolation of her Aunt Schatzi's mountain home in the Smoky Mountains hoping for a quiet retreat. Christmas is approaching, but instead of bringing joy, the holiday season brings memories that intensify Maddie's loneliness. Snowed in and surrounded by a winter wonderland, she begins to confront the grief that has left her feeling stuck in the past, and the strained relationship with her sister that needs to change.

With the warmth of her aunt's straightforward wisdom and the quiet companionship of a helpful neighbor, Sam Bishop, Maddie starts to rediscover the simple beauty of life, love, and family. As the snow falls and the fireside glows, Maddie reflects on her past, healing old wounds, and opening her heart to the unexpected.

When Hannah, a shy teenage girl with her own secrets, comes to them for help, Maddie and Schatzi quickly open their hearts and home. Together, they face life's uncertainties, offering support, laughter, and love as they build a unique family.

This heartwarming Christmas story about love lost and found, the strength of family, and the quiet magic that winter and the holiday season can bring, proves that the light of love can lead us home and help us heal.

Chapter One

The winding mountain road stretched ahead of Maddie, each sharp turn making her grip the steering wheel a little tighter and her knuckles turn white. Thankfully, each bend brought her closer to Aunt Schatzi's house, nestled deep in the Smoky Mountains near Pigeon Forge, Tennessee.

It was a beautiful piece of God's country, but a bit on the remote side. So much so that the GPS had lost its signal twenty minutes ago, but Maddie knew the way. She'd been coming here with Jack for years. Had been.

Before...everything. Before his health had declined, before his heart attack, before the long, silent months that followed, and before the ache of his absence had settled permanently into her chest.

A sudden pang of grief hit her, and Maddie blinked hard, refusing to let the tears come. She cracked the window a few inches and the cold wind rushed in, biting at her cheeks and bringing with it a faint scent of wood smoke, the clean tang of pine, and the earthy smell of fallen leaves.

Somewhere along the way, she had missed the first snow,

but now, tiny flurries swirled around her car, the beginnings of what looked to be a full-on blizzard.

Her older sister, Becca, had called her earlier in the day—an attempt, Maddie supposed, to check in. But Maddie knew that Becca had barely enough time to get through the pleasantries before needing to rush off again.

Becca's life was nothing but a whirlwind of schedules and appointments. Married to a prominent surgeon, Becca's days were filled with dinner parties, charity events, and keeping up with her two grown sons, both of whom lived close to home and seemed to have inherited their father's ambition and drive.

Becca's voice had been warm but distracted, as usual: *"You sure you don't want to come here for Christmas? It'd be good for you, Maddie. I can get Trip to rearrange his schedule, and the boys are dying to see you."*

Rearrange his schedule. That was Becca's world. Everyone's life meticulously ordered by time slots and agendas.

Maddie had declined. Becca's version of Christmas didn't feel like the right place for her, not this year. She didn't have the energy to plaster on a smile and pretend she wasn't still reeling from Jack's death. Becca hadn't really pressed, though. There wasn't time to delve into Maddie's feelings when there were more important things to handle.

The thought of her sister's busyness left Maddie feeling even more alone as she navigated the final twists in the road. No, Aunt Schatzi's was where she needed to be. Her aunt actually wanted her to come, and Maddie knew Schatzi could use the help.

Maddie had tried to find a radio station with a weather report earlier, but the mountains made the stations go in and out. She'd finally given up, deciding that concentrating on her driving was a better idea.

As she rounded the final bend, the house came into view, perched on a hill with a view of the sprawling, snow-covered mountains beyond, and the town of Pigeon Forge in the distance below. The town was nearly invisible because of the snow in the air.

But the sight of the homestead made Maddie's breath catch. The mountain house hadn't changed a bit—the weathered cedar siding, the wide front porch with its matching black rocking chairs, and the stone chimney that seemed to lean a little more each year. It was exactly as she remembered, down to the overgrown bushes that crept along the sides of the house, stubbornly defying the cold.

Pulling up in front of the porch, Maddie killed the engine and sat for a minute, letting the quiet of the place settle over her. The sound of the wind rustling through the trees was the only noise, aside from her own shallow breathing. The smell of damp earth and wood smoke lingered in the air. Maddie put the window up, and as she stepped out of the car, the cold hit her like a wall, sharp and biting.

"Maddie!" Aunt Schatzi's voice called from the porch as she opened the door and stepped out. Her figure was tall and trim, although a little more stooped than Maddie remembered. At the moment, Schatzi was bundled in a thick wool coat, her gray hair poking out from under a knitted cap. She leaned heavily on a cane, though she waved it enthusiastically in Maddie's direction.

Maddie hadn't remembered her needing a cane. The obvious signs of her aunt's aging tugged at her. Life was so unfair in so many ways.

Maddie put on a smile, grabbed her purse and her big suitcase, and lugged the latter up the steps, where the familiar creak of the porch greeted her.

"Hi, Aunt Schatzi," Maddie said, pulling her aunt into a gentle hug. Schatzi smelled of lavender soap and something comforting, like old books and lemon polish.

"You made it just in time," Schatzi said, moving back to

study Maddie with sharp blue eyes. "The snow's coming in fast. They're predicting six inches by morning."

Maddie looked out at the sky, already darkening despite the early hour. The snow was falling steadily now, the flakes swirling in the wind. "Looks like we're snowed in for Christmas," she said, trying to keep her tone light.

"That's all right. You're staying here, so you're exactly where you're supposed to be," Schatzi replied firmly, ushering her inside with a wave of her cane. "Now let's go in. It's freezing out here and I've got lunch just about ready."

Inside, the warmth hit Maddie immediately, the smell of fresh bread and chicken soup wafting from the kitchen. The house felt like a time capsule—nothing had been altered since her last visit years ago.

The same knitted blankets draped the back of the couch, the same cluttered bookshelves lined with old mysteries and family photo albums. The same rough-hewn wood mantel with its array of knickknacks and framed pictures of friends and family.

For some people, seeing nothing had changed might have been disappointing, but to Maddie, all that sameness was like a salve on her soul. She couldn't help but wonder if Becca ever missed this kind of simple comfort, or if she was too caught up in the whirl of her own perfect life to even think about it.

The fireplace crackled, sending waves of heat into the room, and the light from the windows was soft and muted, reflecting the grayness of the world outside.

"Take your coat off and sit down," Schatzi instructed, moving toward the kitchen. "I've got soup on the stove and bread that should be ready any minute."

Maddie shrugged off her coat and hung it on a peg by the door next to her aunt's coat, feeling the warmth of the fire seep into her skin. She walked over to the kitchen doorway. "You didn't have to go through the trouble," she said.

"Nonsense," Schatzi called back, her voice muffled as she bent to check the oven. "Nothing better than homemade bread. Besides, I know you don't eat enough these days. I can see it on you, all that worry you carry around. It's made you thin. Too thin."

Maddie opened her mouth to protest, but before she could, a large orange tabby wound its way between her legs. "Well, hello," she murmured, reaching down to scratch behind his ears. "You're not too thin, are you?" she whispered with a smile.

The cat's fur was warm and soft beneath her fingers, and his loud purring filled the quiet space. He leaned hard into Maddie's hand, closing his eyes in obvious pleasure.

"That's Ernie," Schatzi said, straightening up with a loaf pan of hot bread in her oven mitts.

"Ernie?" That struck Maddie as an odd name for a cat.

Schatzi shrugged. "You don't name cats. They name themselves. You just have to be smart enough to listen when they tell you what it is." Schatzi winked as if making sure Maddie knew she was being funny. "He's been my constant companion since not long after you-know-who left this world."

"Oh." Maddie's heart tightened. Jack had loved Aunt Schatzi's mountain house as much as she did. Every summer, they'd come up here together, hiking the trails, chopping wood for the winter, laughing at her stories, snuggling with mugs of hot cocoa by the fire. Those memories felt distant, like they belonged to someone else.

The sound of Schatzi clattering bowls onto the table pulled Maddie back to the present. "Sit, sit," Schatzi said, waving her over to the table. "I made your favorite soup. Chicken and wild rice."

Maddie sat down, the chair creaking beneath her. She hadn't realized how much she had missed this—warm food, familiar company, the soft glow of a fire on a winter's day. Schatzi set a steaming bowl of soup in front of her, the smell rich and savory, and placed a cutting board with the loaf of bread on the table along with a crock of butter. The golden crust crackled as Maddie tore off a piece.

Maddie dipped the bread into the soup and took a bite. The warmth spread through her, the taste of the broth comforting in a way she hadn't expected. For the first time in a long while, she felt something very much like peace.

As they ate, Ernie curled up at her feet, his fur brushing against her legs. The storm intensified, the wind howling as the snow fell thicker and faster. The world outside was cold and wild, but inside, the warmth of the fire, the food, and Schatzi's quiet companionship wrapped around Maddie like a much-needed hug.

"Maybe after we eat I should get some more firewood in," Maddie offered.

"No need," Schatzi said. "We're well stocked."

They went back to eating, and Maddie was fine with the silence. The bread and the soup were delicious, really hitting the spot. Since losing Jack, she hadn't done much cooking. It was easier to heat up a premade meal.

Now she remembered why cooking was so much better. Aunt Schatzi's lunch was as good as gourmet.

"So," Schatzi said after a few moments, her tone more serious. "You've been keeping busy?"

Maddie nodded, not trusting herself to speak. Busy wasn't the right word. Surviving was closer to the truth. She had filled her days with as many tasks as possible, trying to keep her mind from wandering back to Jack and the gaping hole his absence had left. She wondered what Becca would say about all of that.

If she even remembered what it was like to stop moving for a moment, to feel the stillness.

Schatzi watched her, her sharp eyes narrowing slightly. "You know, Christmas isn't just about doing things. It's about being present. About feeling the spirit of the holiday. You've got to let yourself feel it again. You've got to get back to feeling what you used to feel."

Maddie swallowed hard. "I don't know if I can," she whispered.

Schatzi reached across the table, her hand warm and dry as it settled on Maddie's. "You'll get there," she said softly. "This house, these mountains, this land—they have a way of bringing you back."

Outside, the wind howled and the snow swirled, but inside the house, surrounded by the comforting sounds of the crackling fire, the soothing aroma of fresh bread, and the quiet companionship of a fat cat and a familiar face, Maddie wondered if maybe Aunt Schatzi was right.

Maybe the mountains did have a way of bringing you back. But would it be enough to help her?

Chapter Two

The next morning, Maddie woke to soft, diffused light filtering through the curtains. For a moment, she wasn't sure where she was. The smell of pine and lavender hung faintly in the air, and from somewhere downstairs came the gentle crackle of a fire and the murmur of soft conversation.

Then it all came back to her: the mountain house, Aunt Schatzi, Ernie, the snowstorm, and the quiet sense of escape she hadn't realized she needed.

She listened for a couple of seconds and smiled. Aunt Schatzi was telling Ernie what a good boy he was.

Still smiling at the sweet exchange, Maddie pulled herself out of bed, the chill in the room nipping at her skin as her bare feet hit the rag rug covering the cold wooden floor. Shivering, a quick glance out the window confirmed what she'd already suspected. The world outside remained blanketed in a thick layer of snow, the mountains rising in the distance like a scene from a postcard.

The sky was a pale blue, the sun reflecting off the snow in

blinding patches. It was beautiful and deeply quiet. The kind of peaceful stillness that came after a storm.

She shed her flannel nightshirt to pull on leggings and a long-sleeve T-shirt, then wrapped herself in a thick cardigan and tucked her feet into slipper socks. Feeling warmer, Maddie made her way downstairs. The welcome scent of freshly brewed coffee mingled with the smoky warmth of the fire and something a little spicy. Cinnamon, maybe? Was there anything better to wake up to on a winter's morning?

When she entered the living room, she found Aunt Schatzi sitting in her chair by the hearth, Ernie sprawled lazily on the rug at her feet, looking more like a bathmat than a house cat.

"Morning, sleepyhead," Schatzi said, looking up from her knitting. "I didn't think you'd sleep so long. Good for you. Must've been that mountain air."

"Maybe." Maddie smiled sheepishly, running a hand through her sleep-mussed hair. "I guess I needed it."

"There's coffee and cinnamon buns in the kitchen. Nothing special—they're out of a can, but they're plenty good."

"I thought I smelled cinnamon. Sounds great." Maddie glanced outside at the winter wonderland. "The snow stopped, huh?"

"For now," Schatzi replied, nodding toward the window. "But we're snowed in. Good thing I had Sam come by yesterday to stack more firewood."

"Sam?" Maddie asked, furrowing her brow. The name wasn't familiar to her.

Schatzi glanced at her with a mischievous glint in her eye. "Sam Bishop. My neighbor down the road. He stops by to help out sometimes, since I can't exactly chop wood myself these days."

"Sam Bishop," Maddie repeated. The name stirred something vague in her memory, but she couldn't place it. Schatzi must have mentioned him before. "I don't think I remember him."

"That's because you two never met. He moved here a couple of years ago, after you and Jack stopped coming up as often." Schatzi's voice softened when she mentioned Jack, but she didn't linger on it. "Nice man. Bit quiet, but nothing wrong with that. Lives by himself with his dog, Fargo. He's not far. Just down the way."

As Schatzi finished speaking, a loud, enthusiastic bark came from outside, followed by the muffled sound of a man's voice. Maddie turned to look out the window, her breath catching slightly as the owner of the voice approached the porch.

He was tall, broad-shouldered, and dressed in a plaid wool jacket, a green scarf wrapped loosely around his neck. His dark hair, streaked with gray, peeked out from under a knit beanie cap. Beside him, a chocolate Lab in a red collar bounded through the snow, tail wagging in wide, happy arcs.

"That's him now," Schatzi said with a grin. "He always checks in after a storm."

Before Maddie could say anything, there was a knock at the door, and Schatzi called out, "Come on in, Sam!"

The door creaked open, letting in a burst of cold air as Sam stepped inside, stomping the snow from his boots. Fargo followed close behind, his fur dusted with white, his eyes bright and curious as he sniffed the unfamiliar air.

"Morning, Schatzi," Sam greeted in a low, pleasant voice. His smile was warm as he closed the door behind him, his gloved hands dusting snow off his jacket. He pulled the gloves off and tucked them in his pocket. "Figured I'd come by and make sure you were all set."

"We're just fine, thanks to you," Schatzi replied. "Sam, this is my niece, Maddie. She's staying with me for the holidays."

Maddie smiled and stepped forward, extending her hand. "Nice to meet you."

Sam's handshake was firm but not overwhelming, his hand warm despite the cold. "Likewise," he said, his brown eyes meeting hers with a kindness that put her at ease. "Hope the drive up here wasn't too bad yesterday."

"It was...interesting," Maddie admitted, the memory of the winding mountain road and the snowstorm still fresh in her mind.

Fargo trotted over to her, nosing at her hand as though demanding attention. Maddie knelt to pet him, running her fingers through his thick, soft fur. The dog wagged his tail furiously, leaning into her touch.

"He likes you," Sam said with a smile, watching the scene unfold. "And Fargo's a pretty good judge of character. He knew your aunt cheated at cards the moment he met her."

Maddie laughed. Schatzi had been known to pull a few tricks on occasion. "He's a beautiful dog. How long have you had him?"

"About three years now," Sam replied, his voice softening slightly as he spoke about his companion. "Got him not long after I moved here. He's been good company."

"I bet." Maddie straightened, the mention of companionship stirring something inside her. Since Jack's death, loneliness had been a constant shadow. She wasn't about to share that with a stranger, but there was something comforting about Sam's quiet presence, his connection to the mountains, and the gentle, caring way he interacted with Schatzi and his obvious affection for his dog. It made her wonder, briefly, what her life would have been like if Jack were still here, or if she'd had the kind of support her sister Becca always seemed to offer...when she had time.

Maddie felt a stab of guilt at that thought. Becca had her own life, her own responsibilities that came with her role as the wife of a successful surgeon. Her schedule was undoubtedly packed tighter than a Christmas stocking. Their conversations were usually rushed, Becca speaking to her from the car or about to head into a charity function, promising to call back later, but often forgetting to do so. It wasn't that Becca didn't care—Maddie knew her sister loved her. But sometimes, love wasn't enough to fill the silence.

And with that thought, Maddie was very happy her aunt had someone like Sam as a neighbor.

"Sam does more than just check in," Schatzi said, giving Maddie a sideways glance. "He's been helping me out a lot since my arthritis got worse. Chopping wood, shoveling snow, fixing the leaky roof—you name it."

"Well, I'm happy to help," Sam said, his tone modest. "It's no trouble. Besides, it's not like I've got much else going on."

Schatzi raised an eyebrow at Maddie, but Maddie wasn't sure what her aunt was implying. That Sam was lonely too? That he was around if she wanted someone to talk to?

Ignoring Schatzi's look, Maddie smiled, grateful for Sam's kindness but not wanting to impose. "It's nice to know you're nearby. I appreciate you helping my aunt."

"It's no problem. If either of you need anything," Sam said, turning toward her, "don't hesitate to ask. It's just me and Fargo down the road, and we don't mind lending a hand. Your aunt knows my number, but I'd probably hear you if you hollered loud enough."

"Thanks." Maddie nodded, though she wasn't sure she'd ever feel comfortable calling for help. Vocally or otherwise. She had spent so long handling things on her own that the idea of relying on someone—even someone as kind as Sam—felt foreign.

"Guess I'd better get back before the snow starts up again," Sam said, glancing out the window. "Got a few things to take care of before it gets worse."

"Thanks again, Sam," Schatzi said, standing up from her chair with a little difficulty. "Stay warm out there."

"Will do," he said, pulling his gloves back on. He gave a small nod to Maddie before heading to the door, Fargo bounding happily after him. The cold rushed in again as they left, and Maddie stood by the window, watching them disappear down the snow-covered path.

"He's a good man," Schatzi said, her voice quiet as she sat back down. "Has his own burdens. Who doesn't? Lost his wife a few years back."

Maddie's chest tightened. She hadn't known that. It explained the quiet sadness she had seen in Sam's eyes. The same sadness she saw every time she looked in the mirror. Grief was a terrible common ground to share, but it had a way of binding people together, even if they didn't realize it at first.

"I can tell," Maddie replied softly, her eyes still on the path where Sam and Fargo had walked. "About the burdens, I mean." The world outside was so quiet, the only sounds the faint whistle of wind and the crackle of the fire behind her.

She looked over at her aunt.

Schatzi didn't say anything else, but her expression was filled with understanding. She picked up her knitting again, her needles clicking softly in the cozy silence of the room.

Maddie turned back to the fire, the warmth of the flames brushing against her face. She hadn't expected the mountains to feel this welcoming, this familiar. But something about the quiet house, the snow-covered trees outside, and the brief connection she'd made with Sam and his dog made her feel like this Christmas wouldn't be as lonely as she'd feared.

Of course, it would be hard to be lonely with Schatzi and Ernie for company, but this house still held some memories that were bound to stir up a lot of emotions.

Deciding to focus on the present, Maddie peeked into Aunt Schatzi's cup. "You want more coffee?"

"I'd love some. Thanks." Schatzi worked the yarn without even looking at it, her years of experience guiding her fingers.

Maddie picked up the cup and went into the kitchen to refill it, then got a cup of coffee and a cinnamon bun for herself. She brought all of it back out to the living room. With a sigh, she sank into the chair across from Schatzi, the soft cushions and warm fire just what she needed. Ernie hopped onto her lap, his fur soft under her hand, his purr making her smile.

As Maddie sipped her coffee and managed a one-handed bite of her breakfast pastry, she realized something she hadn't expected.

Being here wasn't just her filling the space in Aunt Schatzi's house. She was filling the space in her heart. Making new memories. That had to be a step forward, didn't it?

Chapter Three

More snow had fallen overnight, piling up nearly another six inches and covering the landscape in an unbroken blanket of white. The world beyond the windows of Aunt Schatzi's house looked like a snow globe that hadn't yet been shaken—peaceful, pristine, untouched.

Maddie sat at the kitchen table, cradling a warm mug in her hands. The smell of fresh coffee and the breakfast casserole in the oven swirled around her, grounding her in the stillness of the moment as she gazed out at the serene winter wonderland. The warmth from the mug seeped into her palms, offering a brief reprieve from the chill that seemed to linger at the edges of the house, despite the constant fire in the hearth.

"Beautiful, isn't it?" Schatzi said from across the table, breaking the silence. She was wrapped in a thick knit shawl, her hands curled around a steaming cup. The lines on her face were softer in the morning light, though her eyes sparkled with the sharpness that had always defined her.

She'd stopped using her cane. Apparently, that only came out when her arthritis was particularly bad.

Maddie nodded. "It really is. There's something about the mountains, isn't there? Even the quiet feels...different. Bigger, somehow."

"The air's better, I'll tell you that much. It's why I've stayed all these years," Schatzi replied, a fond smile tugging at the corners of her mouth. "You can feel the history here. Every winter storm, every gust of wind—it's all woven into the land. It's good for the soul. Helps you see things clearly. Reminds you of what's important."

Schatzi sipped her coffee. "And what's not."

Maddie wasn't sure if she had reached the point of seeing things clearly or knowing what was and wasn't important, but she could admit there was something comforting about the isolation of the mountains. The grief that clung to her felt a little less suffocating in this place.

The ache of Jack's absence remained with her, as constant as her own heartbeat, but it was muted here, like the sharp edges had been worn down by the rhythm of nature and the warmth of Schatzi's company.

Maybe it was all the open space too. The endless sky and the towering mountains wherever she looked. Gave her a feeling she'd never had in the city. Like she could finally breathe. Like a new part of her had room to open up.

Schatzi shifted in her chair, wincing slightly as she adjusted her shoulder. "Stupid arthritis," she muttered. Then louder, "Don't let me forget. Hannah's coming by today."

"Hannah?" Maddie asked, setting her coffee down.

Schatzi nodded. "She comes once a week or so to help with cleaning and errands. Good worker, nice enough girl, but doesn't say much. Keeps to herself. Suppose most teenagers are like that these days."

"Does she live nearby?" Maddie raised an eyebrow, surprised that Schatzi hadn't mentioned Hannah before.

"Not too far. She walks here. I'm sure her father would

drive her, but he works in town, and he's hardly ever around. Hannah's been doing her best, but you can tell she's struggling a bit. Poor girl lost her mother last year. She's only sixteen and already carrying the weight of the world on her shoulders."

Maddie felt a pang of sympathy in her chest at Schatzi's words. Sixteen was far too young to lose a parent, far too young to bear that kind of pain. Maddie understood that all too well. She had been older when she lost Jack, but grief didn't care about age—it hollowed you out just the same.

"Do you talk to her about it?" Maddie asked quietly.

"I've tried," Schatzi said with a sigh. "But she's a tough one to reach. Comes in, does her work, and leaves. Doesn't say much more than she has to."

A few minutes later, there was a quick knock at the door. Maddie glanced at Schatzi, who nodded. "Probably her."

Maddie got up to answer it.

When she opened the door, the cold air rushed in, raising goosebumps on her skin. Standing in the doorway was a thin, dark-haired girl, her features partially obscured by the thick gray scarf wrapped around her face. She had wide brown eyes, and her cheeks were flushed pink from the cold. An army-green canvas bag hung from her shoulder, and her expression was neutral, almost bored.

"Hi. You must be Hannah," Maddie said, offering a small smile.

Hannah nodded once, her gaze shifting briefly to Maddie before darting away. "Is Schatzi here?"

"She's in the kitchen," Maddie replied, stepping aside to let her in. "Come on in. It's freezing out there."

Hannah stepped inside, carefully wiping the snow from her boots before dropping her bag against the wall, then shrugging off her jacket and scarf and hanging them up.

Beneath the coat, she wore a navy hoodie that had both bleach spots and stains on it, looking very much like it had seen better days. She didn't say anything else as she made her way toward the kitchen, her posture stiff and her movements mechanical, like she was just going through the motions.

"Morning, Hannah," Schatzi called out from her seat, giving the girl a warm smile. "You remember I mentioned my niece, Maddie?"

Hannah glanced at Maddie again, her expression unreadable. "Yeah," she muttered. "I remember." Her gaze moved lower to where Ernie was sitting by Schatzi's feet. "Hey, Ern."

He went right on licking his foot, indifferent to the greeting.

Maddie watched as Hannah silently gathered the cleaning supplies from under the sink. There was something so guarded about her, like she was deliberately keeping the world at arm's length. Her movements were small and very careful, as though she was determined to stay invisible, to avoid any unnecessary interaction.

Maddie wanted to say something to break through the girl's wall of silence, to reach out to someone who was clearly struggling, but she wasn't sure where to start. Or if the girl would even be receptive.

Deciding probably not, Maddie instead busied herself by clearing the breakfast dishes and loading the dishwasher. Hannah moved around the room and Maddie with practiced efficiency, her face blank, her actions precise, but without any real energy behind them.

"Everything okay with you?" Schatzi asked after a few minutes, her voice gentle, but probing. "How's your father?"

Hannah shrugged, her back still turned as she wiped down the countertops. "Same as usual. Dad's working."

Schatzi sighed softly but didn't push any further. Maddie could see the concern etched on her aunt's face, but it was clear that Hannah wasn't in the mood for conversation. From the looks of her, that mood wasn't something she was ever in. She seemed determined to get her work done and leave

After a while, Schatzi stood up from her chair and headed toward the living room, Ernie trailing lazily behind. "I'll be in here if you need me," she called over her shoulder, leaving Maddie and Hannah alone in the kitchen.

The silence that followed was awkward, heavy and thick. Hannah moved from task to task with robotic precision. Maddie wanted to say something, anything, to reach out to the girl who reminded her so much of herself at that age—guarded, withdrawn, and carrying a weight that felt too heavy for her years.

Such was the plight of most teenage girls, but one without a mother must be feeling it even more.

"Do you need any help?" Maddie finally asked, hoping to break the silence.

Hannah glanced at her, her expression unreadable. "No. I'm fine."

Maddie bit her lip, unsure of how to respond. She had been a teenage girl once, after all, and knew that pushing too hard wouldn't get her anywhere. But the protective instincts she had learned over the years—first with Jack, and now with Schatzi—were kicking in. She didn't want to sit by and let Hannah stay closed off, but she also didn't want to scare her away.

After a few more minutes of awkward silence, Maddie tried again. "How long have you been helping Aunt Schatzi?"

"A few months," Hannah replied curtly, still not meeting Maddie's eyes.

"I'm sure she appreciates it. I know I do," Maddie said, trying to sound casual.

Hannah shrugged again, clearly uninterested in continuing the conversation. As if to underline that, she put in earbuds, effectively ending any hope of more discussion.

Maddie sighed to herself, feeling like she was hitting a brick wall. She leaned against the counter, crossing her arms over her chest as she studied the girl. Hannah moved through the kitchen like a ghost, efficient but without energy, like she was somewhere far away in her mind. A sense of sadness clung to her, though she hid it well behind a mask of indifference.

When the clock on the wall eventually chimed noon, Hannah grabbed her coat and bag, clearly ready to leave. Schatzi reappeared in the doorway, smiling at the girl and handing her some folded paper money.

"You take care now, Hannah. Same time next week?" Schatzi asked, her voice filled with motherly concern.

Hannah took the money and pulled her scarf tighter around her neck. "Yeah. See you next week."

"Stay warm out there," Schatzi said.

Hannah gave a slight nod, avoiding eye contact as she slipped out the door. The cold air rushed in again, and then she was gone, swallowed up by the winter landscape.

Maddie stared after her, a heaviness settling in her chest. "She's really struggling, isn't she. Very closed down."

Schatzi sighed, sitting back down at the kitchen table. "She is. Lost her mother, and her father's hardly ever home. Practically a stranger to her now. She doesn't talk about it, though. Just comes in, does her work, and leaves."

"I saw that," Maddie said, shaking her head. "It's hard enough being a teenager. Losing a parent on top of that...I can't even imagine."

Schatzi looked at her niece, her expression soft but thoughtful. "You know, you could be good for her, Maddie. She needs someone who understands."

Maddie looked down at her hands, feeling the familiar pang of her own grief. She hadn't expected to come here and find herself drawn into someone else's pain. She had her own to deal with, her own wounds to heal. But Schatzi was right.

Hannah needed someone. That was clear. Maybe Maddie wasn't the perfect person for the job, but she couldn't just ignore the girl's suffering.

"I'll try," Maddie said quietly, more to herself than to Schatzi.

The snow continued to fall outside, soft and unrelenting, and the house grew quieter as the afternoon wore on. But the thought of Hannah lingered in Maddie's mind, a reminder once again that grief, no matter how different, no matter what the source, had a way of connecting people.

Whether they wanted it to or not.

Chapter Four

The snow had stopped falling by the time the afternoon sun began its slow descent behind the mountains, casting a soft golden light over the white-covered landscape. Maddie stood by the window, watching as the last rays of sunlight danced across the snow. It was breathtaking, the kind of beauty that could almost make her forget her troubles. Almost.

Maddie's thoughts—some about herself, some about her aunt, but mostly about Hannah—were too tangled, too heavy to let her fully escape into the scenery.

Her phone buzzed on the table, jolting her out of her reverie. Becca's name flashed on the screen, and Maddie hesitated, her stomach tightening at the thought of answering. It wasn't that she didn't want to talk to her sister—she did, for the most part—but every conversation with Becca lately seemed to leave her feeling more alone.

More like one of Becca's obligations than someone Becca genuinely cared about. Not a great feeling to get from the person she'd been closest to growing up.

Becca had the perfect life, or at least it seemed that way

from the outside. From her successful surgeon husband and her two accomplished sons to her beautiful house in the suburbs, Becca seemed to have it all.

Ever since Becca had married, there had been this distance between them. It had only gotten worse when Jack had passed. It was almost as if Becca couldn't quite understand the grief Maddie carried. Or maybe Becca just didn't have the time to understand. She was always busy, always rushing through their phone calls with promises of, "I'll call you back when things settle down," although that never seemed to happen.

Maddie glanced over at Schatzi, who was sitting by the fire, her knitting needles clicking softly as she worked. She could hear her aunt's voice in her head, telling her to pick up the phone, that family was important, and that no matter how disconnected she felt from Becca, they needed each other. Maddie knew Schatzi was right, but still, she let the phone buzz until it stopped.

It was just too hard, trying to bridge that gap with Becca right now. Her sister lived in a world of precision and order, a life lived on a schedule where problems had solutions, and where grief was something to be managed and moved past. Maddie lived in a messy reality one day at a time, a place of loss where some wounds didn't heal no matter how much time passed.

Maddie prayed many years went by before Becca had to learn for herself just how impossible it was to manage that kind of grief.

Schatzi must have noticed her hesitation. "Was that Becca?" she asked without looking up from her knitting.

"Yes," Maddie replied softly, sinking into the chair across from her aunt but unable to make eye contact because she felt guilty. "I didn't answer."

"So I noticed." Schatzi raised an eyebrow but didn't press. "She probably just wants to check in."

"I know," Maddie said, twisting a strand of hair around her finger. "But it's hard talking to her sometimes. She doesn't get what it's like to lose the person who's most important to you. To experience that kind of pain. She tries, but..." Her voice trailed off, leaving the unspoken words hanging between them.

Schatzi nodded, her expression thoughtful. "Your sister has her own way of dealing with things, you know that. She may not understand your pain, but that doesn't mean she doesn't care. She just comes at it a different way."

Except, to Maddie, Becca's way felt cold and indifferent. Maddie sighed. "I know. I just...I don't know how to talk to her anymore. Everything feels so surface-level with us. Like we're not even in the same world. Which, I guess, we're not. She's got this perfect life, and I have...whatever's left of mine."

"Well, you're here now," Schatzi said, her voice gentle but firm. "And that's a start. Besides, it's nearly Christmas. 'Tis the season for being understanding and forgiving."

Maddie nodded, though the weight of her fractured relationship with Becca still pressed down on her. It was strange how distance—both physical and emotional—could grow between people who had once shared so much. Maddie knew she couldn't blame Becca entirely for the gap between them. She had pulled away too, unable to let her sister in during the darkest moments after Jack's death.

In Maddie's defense, she hadn't let anyone in. She'd closed herself off from everyone for a while. At the time, it had felt like the only way to deal with the pain she'd been in. Hide away and let herself grieve. Now she wondered about the wisdom of that method.

The sound of a vehicle engine approaching the house pulled Maddie out of her thoughts. She looked out the window and saw Sam's old pickup making its way up the snow-covered driveway, Fargo's head poking out the partially rolled down passenger window.

"He's back," Schatzi said with a knowing smile, glancing over at Maddie.

Maddie couldn't help but smile too. There was something comforting about Sam's presence. He had a quiet strength that reminded her of Jack in some ways—steady, dependable, the kind of person who showed up when you needed them, even if you didn't ask.

A few minutes later, Sam knocked on the door, and Maddie got up to let him in. Fargo bounded in first, his tail wagging wildly as he acknowledged both women with enthusiastic sniffs, little nudges, and, in the case of Ernie, a soft woof of greeting.

"Hey," Sam said, stamping snow off his boots as he stepped inside. "Just wanted to check in, see how you're holding up with all this snow."

"We're doing fine, thanks to you," Schatzi replied from her chair before looking at Maddie. "I think I mentioned Sam's been keeping us stocked with firewood," she explained to her niece.

"You did," Maddie said, going back to her seat.

"I figured I'd bring some more up, just in case," Sam said, his brown eyes meeting Maddie's. "This weather can be unpredictable."

Maddie smiled. "Thanks. We appreciate it."

There was a moment of comfortable silence as Sam took off his gloves and warmed his hands by the fire. Fargo sat at Maddie's feet, his head resting on her lap as she absentmindedly scratched behind his ears.

"How's the road?" Schatzi asked, looking at Sam.

"Not too bad. Still pretty slick, but I've got chains on the tires, so it's manageable." Sam glanced out the window at the last light of day fading into dusk. "Looks like we're in for more snow tonight, though. That time of year, I suppose."

Schatzi nodded. "It is. Nothing to do but hunker down and wait it out."

Maddie found herself watching Sam as he moved to stand by the window, his broad frame silhouetted against the soft glow of the firelight. There was a quiet ease about him that made her feel safe, even though they'd only just met. Maybe it was the way he interacted with Schatzi, the genuine care in his voice, or the obvious bond he had with Fargo, taking him everywhere.

Or maybe it was the simple fact that he showed up, that he was here, offering help without being asked.

It reminded Maddie of how things used to be with Jack— how he was always there, always reliable. She missed that kind of stability in her life. And in instances like this, surrounded by the warmth of the fire and the sound of quiet conversation, she realized just how much she missed having someone to share these simple moments with.

Loneliness, especially around the holidays, was such a real thing. She often wondered how many others were out there feeling the same way she was.

"You're welcome to stay for dinner," Schatzi offered, breaking the silence. "There's plenty of chicken and rice casserole, and I'd feel better knowing you weren't driving back in this mess."

Sam hesitated, glancing at Maddie before replying. "I don't want to impose. I was going to run into town, see what the specials were at the diner."

"Nonsense," Schatzi said, waving a hand. "You're eating here, with us. It's no imposition at all. Besides, we could use some good company. Of course, I'm referring to Fargo."

Sam and Maddie both laughed, and Maddie found herself nodding in agreement. "We'd love to have you."

Sam smiled, his eyes warm and kind. "Well, if you're sure..."

"We're sure," Maddie said, feeling a strange sense of comfort settle over her. She wasn't certain when exactly it had happened, but somewhere between the snowstorm and Sam's quiet presence, she had started to feel a little less alone.

As they sat down to dinner, the conversation flowed easily, the warmth of the food and the fire creating a sense of coziness that Maddie hadn't felt in a long time. Sam talked about his work on the cabin he was fixing up down the road, and Schatzi shared stories from her younger days, her sharp wit and dry humor keeping them both laughing.

Maddie listened, a smile tugging at her lips, but her thoughts occasionally drifted back to Becca. She wondered what her sister was doing right now—probably preparing for another holiday party or dealing with some last-minute crisis at work.

Their lives felt so different, like they were moving in opposite directions. And yet, Maddie couldn't shake the feeling that, despite everything, they needed each other more than ever.

Maybe when dinner was all over, she'd call Becca back. Maybe they'd find a way to bridge the distance that had grown between them. But for now, here in the warmth of Schatzi's house, with Sam sitting across from her and the snow falling quietly outside, Maddie let herself be present. For the first time in a long time, she allowed herself to really be in the moment. To appreciate the people she was fortunate enough to share this meal with.

And that, she realized, was enough.

Chapter Five

The days after Hannah's visit passed quietly, with the snow piling up higher around the mountain house and the winter air becoming more penetrating by the day. Maddie still hadn't returned Becca's call, her mind more interested in helping Hannah than reaching out to her non-understanding sister.

The isolation, which Maddie had once craved, now felt stifling at times. It wasn't that she minded the solitude—she *had* come here to escape—but something about Hannah's quiet pain, coupled with her own impossible-to-shake grief, left her feeling restless.

No matter what book she read, what puzzle she put together, what crossword she tried to solve, what Christmas movie she watched with Schatzi, Maddie couldn't stop thinking about the girl, her eyes dark with untold stories, the weight she so obviously carried on her young shoulders.

It wasn't until the afternoon light began to fade and the familiar chill of early evening settled over the house that Maddie decided to go for a walk. The snow compacted under her boots as she made her way down the path that wound through the forest behind Aunt Schatzi's house.

Someone—Sam, most likely—had sprinkled rock salt over it, making the path navigable. A kindness Maddie was thankful for. The opportunity to get out was a welcome one.

The air was incredible. Fresh and clean, with that unmistakable crispness that only came with newly fallen snow. It was the smell of winter, the kind of cold that stung your lungs when you breathed too deeply, redolent with the scent of pine needles and smoke from distant chimneys.

Maddie stuffed her hands into the pockets of her coat and breathed in deeply, her breath forming clouds in the frosty air. The woods were quiet, save for the occasional rustling of a bird or the soft creaking of snow-laden branches. It felt good to be outside, to stretch her legs and clear her head, even if the cold numbed her nose and cheeks.

Her thoughts, however, kept drifting back to Jack. The mountain air, the snow, the stillness—everything about this place reminded her of him and how much he'd loved it here. They had spent so many winters here together, before everything had changed. She could almost hear his voice, teasing her about how she always complained about being cold, even when bundled up in layers.

They had been happy here. But now, without him, the place felt haunted. Every corner of the house, every path through the woods, held a memory of him, like ghosts lingering just out of sight. The last Christmas they had spent together flashed in her mind—the two of them sitting by the fire in Schatzi's home, Jack's arm draped around her shoulders as they sipped hot cocoa, the smell of pine from the Christmas tree filling the room.

The sound of laughter echoed in her memory, Jack's deep chuckle. She thought about how good it was just to be in his presence, how his company made everything all right.

But just as quickly as the memory came, it disappeared, leaving behind only the cold, awful ache in her chest that had become so familiar.

Maddie stopped walking, her breath coming in shallow puffs as she fought against the flood of emotions threatening to overwhelm her. Why was the ache so bad sometimes? When would she get past feeling his way?

She bent down, scooping up a handful of snow and watching it crumble through her fingers. The cold was sharp against her skin, pulling her back to the present. But even as she stood there, surrounded by the quiet beauty of the snow-covered woods, the weight of the past clung to her, refusing to let go.

Just then, the sound of footsteps crunching through the snow reached her ears. Maddie straightened, wiping her hands on her coat as she turned to see Sam approaching, Fargo bounding through the snow beside him, kicking up drifts of white.

"Evening. Mind some company?" Sam called out, his voice carrying through the stillness of the woods.

Maddie smiled and shook her head as she got her gloves out and pulled them on. "Not at all. Are you the one who put salt down?"

"I am. Figured you or Schatzi might want to get out." Sam joined her, his breath coming out in clouds as he slowed to a stop beside her. Fargo, ever the energetic dog, circled them excitedly before stopping to sniff at a twig sticking out of the snow.

"That was nice of you."

Sam shrugged like it was no big deal and adjusted the collar of his coat. "You walk out here often?"

"Sometimes, but this is my first time this visit," Maddie replied, her voice quieter than she'd intended. "It's...peaceful."

Sam nodded, looking around at the snow-covered trees,

the branches heavy with the weight of winter, the shafts of light cast by the setting sun. "I like it out here too. Reminds me that the world keeps moving, even when everything feels like it's standing still."

Maddie glanced at him, catching the deeper meaning behind his words. She wasn't the only one haunted by the past. Sam had lost his wife, and though she didn't know the details, she could see the grief in his eyes, in the lines around his mouth, how it lingered just beneath the surface.

Grief had a way of leaving its mark on a person.

They stood in silence for a while, the only sound the occasional bark from Fargo as he explored the snowy landscape. The cold crept in, but Maddie didn't mind. The quiet was comforting, and there was something about being with Sam that made the weight on her chest feel just a little lighter.

Maybe it was the shared history of sorrow.

"Schatzi mentioned that you lost your wife, so I'm assuming she told you I'm a widow."

"She did."

"Do you ever..." Maddie began, her voice hesitant. "Do you ever get used to it? The quiet, I mean. From being without them?"

Sam was silent for a moment, his gaze fixed on a gap in the trees where the distant horizon was visible. The sun was sinking lower in the sky and painting the edges of the clouds gold. When he spoke, his voice was low and thoughtful.

"No," he said finally. "You don't get used to it. But you learn to live with it. Some days are easier than others. Some days...the quiet isn't so bad. But there are days when it hits you out of nowhere, and all you want is to hear their voice again. To have one more conversation. One more moment."

Boy, did Maddie feel that. She nodded, understanding more than she wanted to. She had spent the last few years learning how to live with the quiet, with the empty space that

Jack had left behind. But some days, like today, the grief felt as fresh as it had the day she'd lost him.

"I think that's what scares me," Maddie admitted, her voice barely above a whisper. "The idea that I'll never stop missing him."

Sam looked at her then, his brown eyes filled with a kind of quiet understanding. "You won't," he said gently. "But missing him doesn't mean you can't still find happiness. It just takes time."

Maddie bit her lip, feeling the sting of tears threatening to rise. She hadn't cried in front of anyone in a long time. She had learned how to keep her grief private, how to hide the pain behind a mask of strength. But standing here, in the middle of the snow-covered woods, with the cold biting at her skin and Sam's quiet, steady presence beside her, she felt the walls she'd built around herself begin to fracture.

"Sometimes I wonder if I even remember how to be happy," she confessed, her voice trembling as she fought her emotions.

Sam didn't say anything for a long moment, his gaze shifting back to the woods around them.

When he spoke, his voice was soft, almost lost in the cold air. "Happiness doesn't have to be big, Maddie. It doesn't have to be some grand thing. It can be a small thing—a walk in the snow, a cup of coffee in the morning, the way the fire crackles when you're sitting near it. Sometimes, it's just about finding the little things that remind you life is still worth living."

Maddie swallowed hard, letting his words settle over her. She hadn't thought about happiness in such a long time, hadn't allowed herself to even consider it. Happiness after losing Jack felt traitorous, even though she knew Jack would want her to be happy. But maybe Sam was right. Maybe happiness didn't have to be something she chased. Maybe it was something she could find in the quiet moments, in the small things.

"I'll try to remember that," she said softly, her breath coming out in a little breath of icy vapor.

Sam nodded, a faint smile tugging at the corners of his mouth. "Good. Because you deserve it. We all do."

They stood in silence for a few more minutes, the sky darkening around them as the sun dipped lower behind the mountains. Fargo trotted over, his nose wet and cold as he nudged Maddie's hand, and she scratched behind his ears, wishing she could feel the softness of his fur, but her gloves prevented that.

Sam cleared his throat. "I should probably get back before it gets too dark. But if you ever want company on one of these walks..."

Maddie smiled, the warmth of his offer chasing away some of the lingering chill. "I'll keep that in mind."

As Sam and Fargo made their way back down the path, Maddie stood still for a few more moments, watching as their figures disappeared into the trees. The cold had seeped deep into her bones, but she didn't feel as alone as she had before.

Turning to head back to the house, Maddie let herself breathe in the peacefulness of the mountains. The snow crunched beneath her boots, the air carried the aroma of someone's delicious dinner being cooked nearby, and, off in the distance, an owl hooted.

She didn't know what the future held, but for the first time in a long time, Maddie felt like maybe, just maybe, there was room for something more in her life—something beyond the grief, beyond the loss.

There had to be, because what kind of existence was she facing otherwise? As she made her way back to Aunt Schatzi's warm, welcoming house, she let herself hope while also reconsidering her reluctance to call Becca.

Chapter Six

Sitting in a chair by the window in her bedroom, Maddie stared at the phone for what felt like an eternity, her finger hovering over Becca's name on the screen. One tap and the phone would dial. The memory of the earlier ignored call lingered, that gnawing sense of guilt creeping back in. She knew it was time to do something about that guilt. To stop avoiding Becca.

After all, Schatzi had been right—family was important, even if it sometimes felt like they were miles apart emotionally.

Taking a deep breath, Maddie pressed the call button, bracing herself for whatever was about to follow. The phone rang only twice before Becca's familiar voice came through, a little breathless.

"Maddie? Hey! I was just thinking you didn't want to talk to me." Becca's laugh was light, maybe a little forced, but Maddie could hear the tension beneath it. Her sister had actually thought Maddie was dodging her.

Maddie felt worse than she had a second ago because that's exactly what she had been doing.

"Yeah, sorry. Things have been...kind of intense lately,"

Maddie said, trying to find the words. She swallowed hard, feeling the familiar lump of grief rise in her throat. "Being at Aunt Schatzi's has brought a lot of memories back."

"I bet," Becca said. Somewhere in the background, a small dog barked. Becca's Yorkie, no doubt, Little Bit. "Hush, Bitty," Becca called out, her voice slightly muffled, probably from her hand over the phone.

Maddie cleared her throat. "Well, um, I just thought it was time we talked."

There was a pause, the silence between them stretching before Becca spoke again, her voice softer this time. "It's okay. I've been busy, as usual. You know how it is. So many last-minute Christmas things to do. Plus, I figured you were going through a lot and probably needed space."

Maddie's lips twisted into a sad smile. *Space* was an understatement. She'd spent the last year putting as much distance as she could between herself and the rest of the world, burying herself in her grief and pushing away anyone who tried to reach out. Including Becca.

"I thought I did, but I'm not sure it was really the best way to handle things. Anyway, I'm sorry for being so distant," Maddie said, her voice breaking a little. "I guess I just didn't know how to talk to you about everything that was going on."

"About...Jack?" Becca's voice was tentative, like she was afraid of saying the wrong thing.

"Yes. About Jack." Maddie exhaled a shaky breath. "I didn't want to burden you with all of that. I know your life is busy and full, and I just didn't think you'd understand. To be honest, I didn't think you *could*."

There was a long silence on the other end of the line, and Maddie could almost hear Becca processing what she had said. Finally, Becca spoke, her voice low and uncertain.

"Maddie, I— Why would you think I wouldn't understand? That I couldn't?"

Maddie hesitated, trying to best untangle her thoughts and put them into words. "Because your life is perfect, Becca. You have everything figured out. You have Trip, the boys, your charity work. You've always had it all together. And I don't. In fact, I'm not sure I'll ever be able to. Not since Jack died."

"Maddie—"

But Maddie's emotions rose in her chest, the weight of all the words she had been holding back for so long pressing down on her. She had more to say. More to confess. "I haven't moved on. I don't know how. It's like I'm stuck in this place where everything reminds me of him, but he's not here. And every time I think I'm starting to get better, something pulls me right back down. A scent, a snippet of memory, a song on the radio. It could be anything. And I know you're trying to help, but you don't get it, Becca. You can't, because you've never had to go through this."

Her voice cracked on the last word, the grief spilling out in a way it hadn't before. A tear slipped down her cheek. She had never said it out loud like this, never let herself admit how truly broken she felt. And as soon as the words were out, she felt both exposed and strangely relieved.

"Maddie..." Becca's voice was barely a whisper. There was another long pause before she continued, her words slow and deliberate. "I'm so sorry. I honestly didn't realize. I just thought you needed time."

Maddie closed her eyes, tears stinging at the edges. "Time isn't enough. I can't just move on like nothing happened. Jack was my life. He was everything to me. And now he's gone, and I don't know how to live without him. I'm trying but it's really hard."

Becca's voice softened even more. "Oh, Maddie. I'm so sorry. I know I haven't lost someone like Jack, but if it helps, my life isn't as perfect as you think."

Maddie blinked, taken aback by the admission. "What do you mean?"

Becca let out a shaky breath, and Maddie could hear her shifting on the other end of the line, like she was finally letting her guard down. "I mean it's not what it looks like. Trip and I —We've been having problems for a while now. He's so busy with work, and when he's home, it's like he's not really *here*. And I'm always trying to keep everything together for him and especially the boys, when they're around, but I feel like I'm losing myself in the process. Half the time, I don't even know who I am anymore outside of being Trip's wife and Ben and Tim's mother."

Maddie's heart sank. She had always envied Becca's life, seeing it as the pinnacle of success and stability. But now, hearing her sister's voice laced with vulnerability, Maddie realized she had been wrong. Becca's life wasn't perfect. It wasn't easy. And she had been struggling in her own way, just as Maddie had been.

"I didn't know," Maddie whispered, her throat tight with emotion.

"How could you?" Becca replied, her voice trembling. "I've never really talked about it with anyone. It's like I've been pretending everything's fine because that's what I'm supposed to do. And if I pretend long enough, maybe it *will* be fine. But the truth is, I know that's not true, and I'm scared. Scared that one day, Trip's going to wake up and realize I'm not enough. That our marriage isn't enough. I feel like I'm always running, trying to keep everything perfect, but it's exhausting, Maddie. It's so utterly exhausting."

Maddie leaned back in her chair, feeling the weight of her sister's words settle over her. It was like they had both been living in these parallel worlds of heartache and struggle, each too afraid to let the other in. But now, with their walls crumbling, they were finally seeing each other clearly for the first time in years.

Schatzi was right about it being the season for such things.

"I'm really sorry, Becca," Maddie said quietly. "I should have been there for you. I didn't realize you were going through all of that."

"There's no way you could have known. And I should have been there for you," Becca said, her voice thick with emotion. "I should have tried harder to understand what you were going through with Jack. I just didn't know how to help, but that's no excuse. You're my sister. I need to do better."

"So do I for you." Maddie nodded, even though her sister couldn't see it. She sniffed. "I don't think either of us knew what to do. But maybe we can figure it out together. I miss you, Becca."

"I miss you too, Mads," Becca whispered, using the nickname from their childhood. Maddie could hear the tears in her voice. "More than you know."

For a few moments, neither of them spoke, the silence filled only with the sound of their quiet breaths. It was a silence that didn't feel awkward or heavy, but full of understanding—a shared acknowledgment of the burdens they had been carrying alone for too long.

Maddie broke the silence first, her voice soft but full of resolve. "Maybe we can start over. Or start fresh. I'm up here with Aunt Schatzi for a little while, just trying to clear my head. But there's no reason we can't talk while I'm here. Really talk. About everything. I know Christmas is a busy time for you, so you just let me know when it works for you, and I'll make sure to be available."

"I'd like that," Becca said, her voice full of relief. "I'd really like that. I'll look at my schedule and text you."

"Good." Maddie smiled, feeling something shift inside her. The grief was still there—it always would be—but having her sister back in her life went a long way toward making her not feel so alone. She had lost Jack, yes. But she still had her sister. And that, she realized, was something worth holding on to.

"Thank you for calling me back," Becca said after a moment. "I know it wasn't easy."

"No, it wasn't," Maddie admitted, wiping a tear from her cheek. "But I'm glad I did."

They talked for a little while longer, the conversation flowing easier, the tension between them finally starting to lift. Maddie filled Becca in on how Schatzi was doing, about Ernie, and Hannah.

She mentioned Sam, but not by name, just referring to him as a helpful neighbor. For reasons of her own, Maddie didn't want Becca to think there was anything more than a friendship there.

Becca updated Maddie on her nephews, telling Maddie all about what the two boys were up to. Maddie decided right then to send them something for Christmas. A little gift basket of sweet treats would be easy enough and it was high time she was part of her nephews' lives again.

By the time they said goodbye, Maddie felt a sense of peace she hadn't known in months. There was still a long road ahead, but at least now she knew she didn't have to walk it alone.

As Maddie put her phone down and looked out at the snow-covered mountains, she felt a weight lift off her shoulders. The grief remained, like a familiar ache, but it didn't feel quite so suffocating anymore. Could it be that she was ready to start healing?

Maybe. The best part was, she didn't feel like she would have to do it all on her own.

Chapter Seven

The early morning light streamed through the windows, casting long shadows across the living room as Maddie sat by the fire, staring into the crackling flames. She'd added a log as soon as she'd come down, giving the embers a stir to get it going again.

She had slept fitfully, her conversation with Becca replaying in her mind over and over. It had felt like a release, finally saying out loud the things she had kept bottled up inside. And hearing about Becca's own struggles had been a shock, reminding Maddie that no one's life was as perfect as it seemed.

But now, in the quiet stillness of Aunt Schatzi's house, Maddie couldn't help but feel a pang of regret for letting so much time pass, for allowing the distance between her and Becca to grow so vast. She wondered how things had gotten so bad between them, and if it was too late to truly fix it.

The soft creak of floorboards interrupted her thoughts, and Maddie looked up to see Aunt Schatzi shuffling into the room, a thick wool cardigan, most likely one she'd knitted herself, wrapped tightly around her narrow frame. She moved slowly, but there was still a strength in her, a quiet resilience that Maddie admired.

"Morning, sweetheart," Schatzi said, giving her a warm smile as she settled into the armchair across from Maddie. "You're up early."

Maddie nodded, running a hand through her tousled hair. "Woke up and couldn't go back to sleep. You want some coffee? I'll get it."

"Sure, that would be great."

Maddie hurried to the kitchen and got her aunt a mug, fixing it just the way she liked it. She brought it out and handed it to Schatzi, who eyed her carefully, as if sensing there was more to Maddie being up early than a restless night.

Schatzi took a sip, then said, "Something on your mind?"

Maddie hesitated, her thoughts drifting back to the phone call with Becca. "I talked to Becca yesterday. It was...good, I think. We talked about Jack, and about her marriage. It turns out her life isn't as perfect as I thought."

Schatzi didn't say anything at first, just nodded slowly as she processed Maddie's words. After a moment, she spoke, her voice gentle but firm. "You know, Maddie, things between sisters are never simple. We expect so much from each other— sometimes too much. It's easy to feel disappointed when those expectations aren't met."

Maddie sighed, leaning back in her chair. "I know, but it feels like Becca and I have been living in different worlds for so long. We don't know how to talk to each other anymore. Although we're working on it."

Schatzi tilted her head, her eyes softening. "You're not the first set of sisters to feel that way. Your mother and I...well, we weren't always as close as we should've been."

Maddie blinked in surprise. "You and Mom? I always thought you two were so close. You always seemed like best friends."

Schatzi gave a wry smile, shaking her head. "We got there, eventually. But it wasn't always easy. Your mother—she was a lot like Becca—always put together, always trying to keep everything perfect and mostly doing it. And me? I was the black sheep, the one who moved to the mountains while she stayed in the city, got married, raised a family, did everything that was expected of her and more. We didn't understand each other for a long time."

Maddie leaned forward, curious. "What happened? Why were things so bad between you?"

"I don't know if bad is the right word, but..." Schatzi sighed deeply, her eyes clouding with old memories. "We had different ideas about life. Your mom thought I was irresponsible, running off to live out here on my own. She wanted me to settle down, find a husband, have kids. She didn't get why I would choose this life. We argued about it nearly every time we talked. She thought I was throwing my life away. That I was being selfish."

Maddie frowned, trying to imagine her mother and Schatzi at odds. It seemed so foreign. Her memories of them weren't like that at all. "How did you make peace with each other?"

"It took time," Schatzi admitted. "And distance. We didn't speak for nearly two years at one point."

"Two years?" Maddie's mouth hung open.

"Yep. I was too stubborn, and so was she. But eventually...well, life has a way of reminding you about what's important. Your mom came up here one summer after she'd gone through a rough patch. She didn't say much about it, but I could tell she was struggling. Her marriage was rocky, and I think she was feeling overwhelmed with all the pressure she put on herself."

"I don't remember that."

"It was right after you and Becca were born. You were a

baby and Becca was just a toddler." Schatzi paused, her expression softening as she remembered. "We sat out on this porch one evening, watching the sunset, and for the first time, she really opened up to me. She told me how hard it was trying to keep everything perfect for you girls, trying to be the perfect wife and mother. And I finally realized...she wasn't judging me because she thought I was wrong—she was just scared. Scared that she'd lose control of her own life if she didn't hold on so tightly."

Maddie swallowed, her heart aching at the thought of her mother carrying that kind of burden. She had never seen that side of her before, the side that felt unsure or overwhelmed. But, boy, did Becca take after her.

Schatzi continued, her voice gentle. "That's when I understood that no matter how different we were, we were still sisters. Family. We needed each other, even if we didn't always get along. That night, we stopped trying to fix each other. We just accepted that we both had our own paths to walk."

Maddie looked down at her hands, feeling a lump forming in her throat. "I never knew that about you and Mom."

Schatzi smiled sadly. "We didn't always talk about it, but it's true. And that's why I'm telling you now, Maddie—don't let too much time pass with Becca. Don't wait for some crisis to remind you of what's important. She's your sister. You don't have to understand each other all the time, but you do need each other. Just being there is sometimes all that matters."

Maddie felt a tear slip down her cheek and quickly wiped it away. Schatzi was right—she had been so caught up in her own grief and frustration that she had shut Becca out. And in doing so, she had only deepened the distance between them. Becca had her own struggles, just like their mother had, and Maddie had been too blind to see it.

"I feel like I've been so selfish," Maddie whispered, her

voice thick with emotion. "I've been so focused on my own pain that I didn't even think about what Becca might be going through."

Schatzi reached across to the other chair, taking Maddie's hand in her own. "Grief makes us selfish sometimes and that's okay, as long as we recognize it. Don't blame yourself. It's not your fault. But now that you know better, you can do better. You've still got time to make things right with Becca."

"Yeah." Maddie squeezed her aunt's hand, the warmth of the contact comforting her. "I talked to her yesterday. Really talked to her for the first time in a long time. She told me about her marriage, how hard it's been."

Schatzi nodded knowingly. "See? She's carrying her own burdens, just like you. You two might be more alike than you realize."

"I thought that too." Maddie smiled through her tears, feeling a strange sense of relief wash over her. For so long, she had seen Becca as this untouchable figure, someone who had it all together, while she herself had been falling apart. But maybe they weren't so different after all. Maybe they were just two sisters, both trying to navigate the messiness of life in their own way.

"I think you're right," Maddie said softly. "I need to try harder. I don't want to lose her."

"You won't," Schatzi said firmly. "You've already taken the first step. The rest will come in time."

Maddie wiped her eyes, feeling lighter than she had in months. She thought about Becca, about their shared childhood, about all the things that had pulled them apart and the things that bound them together. For the first time, she truly understood how important it was to keep those bonds intact.

"I'm going to call her again today," Maddie said with quiet determination. "I want her to know I'm here for her."

Schatzi smiled, the kind of smile that said she was proud,

but not surprised. "Good. I think you'll find that once you open that door, things will start to get better."

Maddie nodded, a small, hopeful smile forming on her lips. She glanced out the window, the morning light casting a soft glow over the snow-covered mountains. The world outside looked still and peaceful, but Maddie knew now that life was never as simple as it seemed.

But that was okay. Because she wasn't alone in it. Not anymore.

And as long as she had her sister, she never would be.

Chapter Eight

The snow had let up by the end of the week, leaving the mountains draped in a thick blanket of white. The air, crisp and biting, carried the unmistakable scent of woodsmoke, drifting from chimneys hidden among the trees.

Maddie stood by the front window, watching the last rays of sunlight dip below the snow-capped peaks. The world outside seemed frozen in time, the only sound the occasional creak of the house settling against the cold.

Behind her, Aunt Schatzi was moving about the kitchen, the clatter of pots and pans breaking the silence. The warmth from the fireplace made the air inside the house feel heavy, but comforting, like being wrapped in a well-worn quilt. Maddie leaned her forehead against the cold window, her breath fogging up the glass as she thought about the evening ahead.

"Maddie, dear," Schatzi called from the kitchen, her voice a little more hurried than usual. Despite her shoulder bothering her, she'd insisted on doing her share of the chores. "Are you sure you're up for this? It's not too late to stay in."

"I'm up for it." Maddie said, though there was a flicker of

uncertainty in her voice. She turned to face her aunt, her fingers still gripping the window frame. Schatzi was fussing with an oversized casserole dish, her one good arm struggling to adjust the lid as she got it out of the dishwasher. Maddie had tried to help but Schatzi wasn't having it, saying she was already doing too much.

"Let me." Maddie crossed the room and gently pried it from her hands, setting it on the counter with a reassuring smile.

"Thanks." Schatzi turned and got a quart of cider out of the fridge. "You're sure about tonight?"

The idea of going to a gathering—a Christmas gathering, no less—still made her chest tighten. But it had been Schatzi's idea, and Maddie didn't want to disappoint her by saying no. "Yes. Besides, I think I need to get out of the house."

Schatzi raised an eyebrow, her sharp eyes twinkling. "A little socializing will do you good, that's for sure. It's mostly just the ladies from around the area and a few of their husbands. They're all good people. You'll like them."

Maddie forced a smile, nodding as she glanced out the window again. The thought of meeting new people, especially around Christmas, made her stomach knot. But maybe it was time. She knew she needed to stop retreating into her shell, but actually doing something about it wasn't so easy to accomplish. The quiet of the mountains had helped, but it was only masking the emptiness inside her, not filling it.

Schatzi grabbed the cider and started for her coat by the door. "Don't worry about a thing. They'll be too busy gossiping and sharing holiday recipes to pay much attention to us."

Maddie, slipping into her coat and wrapping a scarf around her neck, doubted that very much. But she could handle small-talk about baking and town news. It would be easy to smile and nod, to listen without saying too much. At least, she hoped it would. "You want me to carry that jug?"

"No, I can manage it. I'm old, I'm not dead."

"Just trying to help." Maddie thought about taking it anyway, but Schatzi was stubborn and wouldn't appreciate being treated like she couldn't do things for herself, so Maddie let her be.

The walk to the bonfire wasn't far. Schatzi had mentioned that her neighbors, Tom and Alice Parker, hosted a Christmas bonfire on their land down by the frozen creek every year.

As Maddie and Schatzi got closer, the path through the woods was lit by lanterns hanging from low branches, their flickering light casting shadows that danced on the snow-covered ground. The cold air stung Maddie's cheeks, but there was a kind of beauty in the stillness of the evening and the faint crunch of snow beneath their boots.

For a passing moment, Maddie almost felt like she was going to church.

When they reached the clearing, the smell of burning wood filled the air, mingling with the sweet scent of mulled cider that someone had brewed over a camp stove in a big stock pot. Paper cups of it were being passed around. More lanterns, dangling from branches, lit the area.

The bonfire itself roared in the center of the clearing, flames licking toward the night sky, casting a warm glow over the group that had gathered. There were a dozen or so women gathered in a big group, bundled in heavy coats and scarves, their breath fogging in the cold air as they laughed and talked.

The men had formed several smaller groups on the other side of the bonfire.

"Schatzi!" a voice called from near the fire, and an older woman with rosy cheeks and a bright smile waved them over. "You made it! We were beginning to wonder if the snow had kept you in."

"Nothing keeps me in if I can help it," Schatzi replied, her tone as feisty as ever. She leaned in toward Maddie and whispered, "That's Alice Parker. She and her husband own the big cabin up the ridge."

Maddie smiled as Alice greeted them warmly and took the extra cider from Schatzi with a grateful nod. "And you must be Maddie," Alice said, her eyes crinkling with kindness. "We've heard a lot about you."

"All good things, I hope," Maddie replied, forcing a light laugh.

Alice smiled warmly. "Only good things. We're so glad you're here."

"Thanks." The warmth of Alice's welcome eased some of Maddie's tension, and as they moved closer to the fire, the others gathered around to introduce themselves. There was Beth, a retired schoolteacher who seemed to know everything about everyone in town; Junie, a younger woman with two small children who were already asleep back at the house with her husband; and Lyla, a hairdresser in town whose makeup looked like something off a magazine cover.

The conversations flowed easily, touching on everything from the weather to Christmas traditions to how much shopping they all had left to do, and for the first time in a long while, Maddie felt herself relax.

But as the evening wore on, Maddie found herself standing slightly apart from the group, watching the flames dance and crackle. The warmth of the fire seeped into her bones, and the smell of burning wood brought back a flood of memories. Mostly Christmases spent here with Jack. They'd never come to this gathering, but a few of the faces still looked familiar.

She was sure they all knew Jack had died. Schatzi would have told them. Thankfully, no one had said anything about him. She wasn't sure she could bear to talk about him without breaking down.

Her throat tightened as she thought of his easy smile, the way his arm would always drape around her shoulders, pulling her close. Not even the good memories were grief-free these days.

"Hey, there."

Maddie turned to see Sam Bishop standing beside her, a paper cup of steaming cider in his hand. Fargo sat at his feet, his eyes fixed on the fire, content to be close to his owner.

"Sam," Maddie said, surprised but pleased to see him. "I didn't know you were coming tonight."

He smiled, his breath forming small clouds in the cold air. "Alice always ropes me into these things. She's impossible to say no to." He took a sip of cider before adding, "Besides, it's tradition. You want some cider?"

"No, I had some. Thanks." Maddie turned back to the fire. The orange and red flames swayed against the dark backdrop of the woods, casting a glow on the faces of those gathered around. There was something mesmerizing about it, something soothing in the way the fire consumed the wood, crackling and popping as it burned.

"How're you holding up?" Sam asked, his voice gentle, as though he sensed the swirl of emotions Maddie was trying to keep at bay.

Maddie hesitated, then shrugged. "I'm here," she said, her tone soft. "That's something."

Sam nodded, his expression full of understanding. "That's a lot, actually."

Maddie glanced at him, catching the way the firelight reflected in his eyes. Sam's presence was comforting in a way he probably didn't even realize—he didn't push, didn't pry, but he was there, solid and steady, like the mountains themselves.

"You're not much for these kinds of things either, huh?" Maddie asked, her voice tinged with humor.

Sam smiled faintly, shaking his head. "Not really. But it's good to be around people sometimes. At least, that's what I've been told."

With a little snort, Maddie looked around at the men and women laughing and talking, the warmth of the fire contrasting sharply with the coldness of the night. The dancing shadows turned the snow blue.

She knew he was right. As hard as it was to be out here, surrounded by reminders of the life she used to have, it was better than sitting alone in the dark. And there was something about the mountain community—its quiet strength, its resilience, the open-hearted welcome—that was starting to feel like home.

"You ever think about leaving?" she asked suddenly, the question surprising even herself. She wasn't quite sure where it had come from.

Sam raised an eyebrow. "Leaving?"

"The mountains," Maddie clarified. "All this...quiet."

Sam shook his head, a soft smile playing on his lips. "No. I came here to find the quiet. Sometimes it's the only thing that makes sense. Probably what keeps me sane."

Maddie nodded, his words resonating with her. The mountains *did* make sense. Even in their stillness, even in the snow and the biting cold, there was a kind of peace here—a peace she'd been searching for. She just hadn't known until now it could be found here.

"I think I'm starting to understand that," Maddie said quietly, more to herself than to Sam.

They stood in silence for a while longer, the warmth of the fire flickering across their faces, the sound of the others fading into the background. For the first time in months, maybe even years, Maddie felt something come alive inside her—a sense of possibility, of life continuing, even after everything had changed.

Fargo nudged her hand with his nose, breaking her reverie. She smiled and pulled off one glove, kneeling to scratch behind his ears, feeling the softness of his fur against her cold fingers. "Hiya, buddy. You certainly like people, don't you?"

"Well, he certainly likes you," Sam said with a chuckle.

"I like him too," Maddie replied, standing back up. The warmth of the fire felt good, but it was the warmth of the company that truly thawed the ice in her heart.

As the evening wound down, Schatzi caught Maddie's eye from across the fire and gave her a knowing smile. Maddie returned the smile, feeling something well up in her that she hadn't expected: hope.

Hope that maybe this Christmas, despite everything, she could begin to heal.

Hope that the mountains, with their quiet strength, might just be the place where she found herself again.

And wouldn't that be a miracle?

Chapter Nine

Maddie was wiping down the kitchen counter after breakfast the next morning when she heard a sound that nearly stopped her heart—a loud crash followed by a sharp cry of pain and a scared meow. Her heart lurched, and the dish towel dropped from her hands.

"Aunt Schatzi?" she called out, her voice tight with fear as she rushed toward the sound.

Rounding the corner into the living room, she found Aunt Schatzi crumpled on the floor near the staircase, her face pale, her breath coming in quick, shallow pants. Her cane lay on the floor beside her, and her right arm was bent at an unnatural angle. Ernie, the ever-watchful orange tabby, stood nearby, his tail twitching nervously.

"Oh, no, Schatzi!" Maddie gasped, dropping to her knees beside her aunt. "What happened?"

Schatzi winced, clutching her arm. "I—ugh. I missed the last step. I grabbed the railing, but my shoulder went wonky. Stupid, stupid. My arm... It's bad, Maddie."

Maddie's hands hovered, unsure of where to touch her aunt without causing more pain. Schatzi's skin was clammy, her forehead damp with sweat. Her breathing was shallow, and her face twisted with pain every time she tried to move.

"Okay, we need to get you to a doctor. Or, better yet, the emergency room. Or is there a clinic?" Maddie's voice was shaking. She gently touched Schatzi's good arm, trying to keep her calm. "I'll call Sam. He can help us get you there."

Schatzi's face contorted in frustration. "No need to fuss. Feels like a stupid dislocation. I've had worse."

Maddie wasn't convinced. Schatzi was tough, but the way her arm hung unnaturally and the paleness of her face told Maddie it was serious enough to warrant professional care. "You're not going to argue with me on this one, Aunt Schatzi. I'll be right back."

Maddie scrambled to her feet, grabbed her aunt's phone from the kitchen counter, and quickly scrolled to Sam's number. She hadn't wanted to rely on him so soon, but right now, she didn't see another choice. Her fingers trembled as she pressed the button to call him.

She started talking as soon as he answered. "Sam? It's Maddie. I need your help—Schatzi fell, and I think she dislocated her shoulder. I can't get her to the clinic by myself."

"I'll be right there," Sam's calm voice responded almost instantly.

Within minutes, Maddie heard the sound of tires on the snow outside and the low rumble of Sam's truck coming to a stop. Fargo barked once, announcing their arrival.

Maddie rushed to the door and flung it open just as Sam stepped out of his truck, his expression deep with concern. "Where is she?" he asked as he headed toward the house.

"By the stairs in the living room," Maddie said, stepping aside to let him by. "She's in a lot of pain."

Sam went straight ahead, his boots tracking snow across the entryway as he hurried toward Schatzi. He knelt down beside her, assessing her arm with cautious eyes.

"Schatzi, I'm going to help you up, but we need to be careful, okay?" Sam said gently, his hands steady and sure.

Schatzi nodded tightly, her jaw clenched in pain. "Fine. Just get me off this damn floor."

Together, Maddi and Sam—mostly Sam—managed to carefully lift Schatzi from the floor. Her face was white with pain, and Maddie flinched as she watched her aunt bite back a groan.

"You're doing great, Schatzi," Maddie said, trying to sound reassuring even though her stomach twisted with worry.

Sam guided Schatzi toward the door, his strong arms supporting most of her weight. "Maddie, grab her coat and purse. We'll get her to the walk-in."

Maddie hurried to get Schatzi's coat and purse and went after them. The cold air outside was a shock, the bitter wind stinging Maddie's cheeks. Fargo trotted beside Sam, his brown eyes full of concern, as if he knew something was wrong and wanted to help in any way he could.

Once Schatzi was settled in the passenger seat of Sam's truck with her coat around her, Maddie climbed into the small backseat with Fargo, who curled up beside her, his head resting on her lap. Sam had left the truck running when he'd come inside, so the heat was on.

She absentmindedly stroked Fargo's fur as they drove down the winding mountain road, her pulse still elevated from the sight of Schatzi crumpled on the floor. Thank God it had only been her shoulder.

The drive to the clinic was tense, the truck's tires grinding over the snow-covered road. Sam kept the conversation light, telling Schatzi about a recent project he was working on to repair the roof of the cabin down the hill. Schatzi, despite her obvious discomfort, tried to keep up with the banter, but Maddie could see the pain etched in her face, even in profile.

By the time they arrived at the small clinic in town, Schatzi's skin had gone ashen, and her breaths were shallow. Maddie couldn't imagine the pain she was in.

The nurse, recognizing Schatzi immediately, wasted no time getting her into a room. Maddie started to follow, but Schatzi frowned, despite the pain. "I don't need babysitting," she grumbled.

Maddie sighed at her aunt's crankiness and went back to sit in the waiting area, bouncing her knee anxiously. Sam stood nearby, his hands shoved into his coat pockets as he watched Maddie with concern.

"It's just the pain," he said.

"That and she hates being seen as old and vulnerable. I get it. It's just who Schatzi is."

"Very true. She'll be all right," Sam said quietly, finally taking a seat beside her. "Dislocations are a real bear, but they'll fix her up."

"I hope so," Maddie whispered, staring at the floor, thinking about how she'd found Jack on the floor, too. The thought sent a chill through her. She needed Schatzi more than anything. "She doesn't deserve this."

Sam reached out and placed a reassuring hand on her shoulder, the warmth of his touch bringing her back to the moment. "Schatzi's as tough as they come. She'll be just fine."

Maddie nodded, though the knot of worry in her stomach didn't fully ease. She had always known Schatzi as strong, but seeing her vulnerable like that, seeing her in pain, had shaken something loose inside Maddie. Schatzi wasn't indestructible. None of them were. Jack had proved that. The weight of the realization made Maddie's entire being feel heavy.

While they waited, Maddie sent Becca a quick text. *Schatzi fell and hurt her arm. At the walk-in now. Maybe a dislocated shoulder? I'll keep you posted.*

Becca was quick to respond. *Oh, no! Tell her I'm thinking about her and praying for her. Let me know!*

About an hour later, the doctor came out to meet them, a friendly smile on her face. "Schatzi's shoulder was dislocated, but we've reset it. She'll need to wear a sling for a few weeks and take it easy—no heavy lifting or sudden movements."

Maddie let out a breath she'd been holding. "That's a relief. Can I see her?"

The doctor nodded. "She's in recovery now. She'll be a bit sore, but she's already giving the nurses a hard time," she added with a chuckle. "That woman doesn't like to sit still. That might change once the pain meds kick in."

Maddie smiled, the tension in her chest loosening just a little. That sounded like Aunt Schatzi.

When Maddie entered the room, Schatzi was propped up in a bed, her right arm secured in a sling. She looked pale but alert, her blue eyes sharp as ever.

"See? Nothing to worry about," Schatzi grumbled, though her voice was laced with exhaustion. "Just a bump in the road."

Maddie walked over to the side of the bed and squeezed Schatzi's good hand. "You scared the daylights out of me. And Ernie."

Schatzi's expression softened slightly, though she tried to keep up her tough facade. "Didn't mean to. But I'll be fine, I promise. You can stop hovering."

Maddie shook her head, a mix of relief and exasperation bubbling up. "Hovering is my job now."

Schatzi huffed, her lips twitching with a ghost of a smile. "Lord help me."

Maddie updated Becca by text on the drive home later that afternoon. By the time Sam had them back to the mountain house, Schatzi had resumed her no-nonsense attitude, though she moved a little slower and complained more than usual.

Sam and Maddie helped Schatzi get settled in her favorite armchair by the fire, a warm blanket tucked around her legs, while Ernie jumped up onto Schatzi's lap, purring softly.

Maddie nodded her approval. "He's glad you're home and even more glad you're okay."

Schatzi scratched Ernie's head, smiling at the cat. "I'm all right, boy."

"You sure you're comfortable?" Maddie asked for the third time, fussing with the blanket.

"Maddie, I'm fine," Schatzi said, her tone bordering on irritated. "I'm just a little banged up. I've survived worse winters than this."

Sam chuckled from his spot near the doorway, where Fargo was sitting. "Better get used to it, Schatzi. Maddie's not going to let you lift a finger for a while. Which is as it should be."

Schatzi rolled her eyes, though there was affection in her expression. "Between the two of you, I'll be lucky if I'm allowed to leave this chair."

Maddie smiled, but she couldn't shake the lingering worry. Schatzi was tough, but she wasn't invincible. Maddie knew she'd need to step up in the coming weeks—take care of the house, the errands, and, most importantly, Schatzi.

Maddie would have preferred her aunt to be whole and healthy, obviously, but taking care of someone, having another person to focus on, might be nice for a change.

Sam stepped forward, his presence calm and reassuring. "If you need any extra help, Maddie, don't hesitate to ask. I'm just down the road. You know that."

"I do. I really appreciate it, Sam," Maddie said softly, meeting his steady gaze. His offer wasn't just a polite gesture—she knew that he meant it. What a good man he was.

As Sam turned to leave, a tail-wagging Fargo in tow, Maddie followed him to the door. "I don't know how to thank you," she said, keeping her voice low so Schatzi wouldn't overhear and make any more fuss.

Sam waved it off. "You don't need to. Schatzi's like family to me. I'm just glad I could help."

Maddie hesitated, feeling a warmth in her chest that hadn't been there in a long time. She had spent so long trying to handle everything on her own—her grief, her isolation—but now, standing here with Sam, she realized how silly that was. There were people here who cared, who wanted to help.

"Still," she said quietly, "I don't know what I would have done if you weren't around. You were a huge help."

Sam's smile was gentle, and for a brief moment, Maddie let herself feel the comfort in his presence, in knowing that she wasn't alone in this.

"Anytime," he said before stepping out into the cold, Fargo trotting happily by his side as they walked to the truck.

Maddie watched them go, the rumbling sound of the engine fading into the snowy distance. When she closed the door and turned back to the warmth of the fire and the quiet company of Aunt Schatzi and Ernie, who were both now asleep, she felt something shift inside her.

Almost like she was starting to feel at home again.

Chapter Ten

The days following Schatzi's fall passed in a quiet rhythm. The house, warmed by the crackling fire and filled with the comforting scent of simmering soups and plenty of tea, became a cocoon of healing.

Hannah came and went, quieter and more withdrawn than ever, although she'd taken a moment to ask if Schatzi needed anything extra, then said she hoped Schatzi healed up fast.

Maddie had slipped into the role of caregiver seamlessly, ensuring Schatzi rested as much as possible, even though Schatzi complained constantly about being "babied."

Despite Schatzi's protests, Maddie kept her aunt in that armchair as much as she could, fluffing pillows and fetching blankets, even bringing her a footstool to rest her feet on. Maddie took over Ernie's care, too. Feeding him, changing his water, making sure his litter box was clean. She didn't mind any of it, because it was all for Schatzi.

Schatzi, on the other hand, grumbled, mostly about how frustrated she was not to be able to knit, but there was a hint of gratitude in her blue eyes.

Her stubbornness couldn't entirely mask her pain or the relief she felt in being looked after. Even Ernie seemed to sense it. The orange tabby rarely left Schatzi's lap, curling up like a sentry, keeping her company as the fire crackled nearby.

"Maddie, I'm not made of glass," Schatzi muttered one afternoon, wincing as she shifted in the chair. "You've already done enough fussing for a dozen winters."

Maddie, chopping vegetables for soup, glanced over her shoulder. "It's not fussing. It's called caring."

Schatzi raised a brow. "Same thing, isn't it?"

"Not when it's you," Maddie replied with a grin, focusing on the knife and the rhythmic chop against the wooden board as she finished up the carrots.

Outside, the snow still blanketed the world in silence, but the skies had cleared, revealing a deep blue above the treetops. Maddie's world had felt like that for so long—endless storms, then a stillness that left behind the same cold.

The house, though, was slowly thawing something in her. The warmth of the fire, the closeness of her aunt, the new understanding with Becca, and even Sam's quiet presence in her life had started to melt the frost that had settled in her heart.

Just as Maddie dropped the vegetables into the pot, she heard the familiar sound of boots on snow. Her heart gave an unexpected flutter.

Over the past few days, Sam had checked in regularly, making sure they had enough firewood, offering to help with errands, bringing them some groceries, and generally giving Maddie more reasons to appreciate his steady, kind nature. Fargo was usually with him, trotting along like Sam's shadow, ready to curl up by the fire or nudge Maddie's hand for a pat.

"Sam's here," Schatzi announced from her chair as the knock sounded on the door.

"I heard him." Maddie quickly wiped her hands on a towel

and went to open the door, the cold air rushing in along with Sam and Fargo. Sam's cheeks were red from the cold, but his smile was as warm as ever.

"Morning," he said, glancing between Maddie and Schatzi. "Thought I'd stop by, see if you ladies need anything before I head into town."

Maddie returned his smile. "You're too good to us, Sam."

Schatzi made a huffing sound from her chair. "He's good to *me*," she corrected with a wink. "He just knows you're stubborn and won't ask for help."

Maddie rolled her eyes, though she couldn't deny the truth of it. Asking for help had never been easy for her, especially after Jack. She had become so used to handling everything on her own that accepting help felt like admitting a weakness.

Which was probably its own weakness.

Fargo wandered over to Schatzi's chair and rested his head on her lap, his tail wagging lazily. He sniffed at Ernie. Ernie's head came up and he gave the dog a serious look.

"It's all right, boys. You've known each other too long to get uppity now." Schatzi chuckled and patted Fargo on the head, her fingers trailing through his soft fur.

"How are you feeling today?" Sam asked Schatzi, his gaze assessing as he glanced at her arm in the sling.

"Like I'm being held prisoner," Schatzi replied, though her tone was light. "Maddie's determined to keep me tethered to this chair for the rest of the winter."

"You need to rest, Aunt Schatzi," Maddie said, returning to the stove to stir the pot. The smell of chicken and vegetables had just started to fill the kitchen, making the house feel cozier. She still had to add a cup of barley. She planned to make biscuits for their lunch, too. "The doctor said no heavy lifting."

"That doctor's never met a woman who spent seventy-eighty years in these mountains," Schatzi muttered. "Heavy lifting is in our blood."

Sam chuckled softly as he added a little wood to the fire, shaking his head, no doubt at the two of them bantering. His presence had a way of balancing things, of making the house feel more settled. Maddie found herself increasingly grateful for his quiet company.

"Well, if you need any more supplies, I'm happy to pick them up while I'm in town," Sam said, his brown eyes shifting to meet Maddie's. "Just give me a list."

"Thank you," Maddie replied, her heart warming at his offer as she lowered the temperature on the stove. "I'll make sure we're stocked up before the next snow hits."

Sam gave a small nod, then knelt down to pet Fargo, who'd laid down by Schatzi's feet, perfectly positioned so that Ernie's tail swished over his head. As Sam ruffled the dog's fur, something shifted in his expression—something a bit more serious.

"You know," Sam said, looking up at Maddie, "I ran into Bill, Hannah's dad, in town yesterday."

Maddie turned away from the stove, her brow furrowing at the mention of the closed-off teenager. Hannah, with her quiet demeanor and guarded eyes, had been on Maddie's mind since the girl's last visit. There was something more going on with the girl, something Maddie couldn't quite put her finger on.

"Her dad?" Maddie asked as she took a few steps toward the living room. "How's he doing?"

Sam gave Fargo one more scratch, then stood up. "He looked...rough, to be honest. Exhausted, mostly. Said he's been working long hours, trying to keep up with things. He can't be home much."

"That poor child," Schatzi muttered, shaking her head. "She's practically raising herself."

"I've been thinking a lot about her," Maddie admitted,

resting her hand on the back of the chair across from Schatzi. "She hardly talks when she's here, but there's something not right. You can just tell. I can't help but worry about her."

"She's holding something back, that's for sure," Sam said, his voice thoughtful. "I've seen her around town a few times. She keeps to herself, doesn't talk to anyone. Barely makes eye contact most of the time."

Maddie felt a knot tighten in her stomach. She had been in Hannah's shoes before, carrying the weight of the world on her shoulders without knowing how to ask for help. It was the same knot she had carried after Jack died. The same knot she still felt at times.

"I'll try talking to her next time she's here, which I think is tomorrow," Maddie said quietly. "Maybe she just needs someone to listen."

Schatzi glanced at Maddie, her expression softening. "You're good at that, you know. Listening."

Maddie smiled faintly, though there was a pang in her chest. Listening wasn't always enough. Sometimes, a person had to act.

The next day, it started snowing again. Lightly. Not nearly enough to keep Hannah away. She showed up as usual, her dark hair hidden beneath a knit beanie, her eyes downcast as she shrugged off her coat. Maddie was in the kitchen, prepping a small roast that would be their dinner, while Schatzi dozed by the fire. Ernie, ever watchful, was curled up in a ball on Schatzi's lap.

"Hey, Hannah," Maddie greeted, keeping her tone light and casual. "Glad you could make it."

Hannah muttered a response, her eyes darting briefly toward Maddie, then to Schatzi, who'd woken up at the sound of the door. "Feeling any better?"

"About the same," Schatzi answered.

With a nod, Hannah got to work, busying herself with the

broom, sweeping the wide wood floorboards with almost mechanical movements.

Maddie chopped up some veggies to go along with the roast, the rhythmic sound of the knife slicing the potatoes into chunks filling the quiet. She kept glancing at Hannah, trying to find an opening, a way to break through the wall the girl had built around herself.

"Hannah," Maddie said after a few minutes, setting the knife down and wiping her hands on a towel. "Can I ask you something?"

Hannah's shoulders stiffened slightly, but she didn't stop sweeping. "What?"

Maddie stepped closer, keeping her voice soft. "Are you okay? I mean, really okay? You seem like something's bothering you and I just want you to know that if you need to talk to someone..."

Hannah stopped sweeping, the broom frozen midmotion. She didn't turn around, didn't meet Maddie's eyes, but the tension in her body was palpable. For several seconds, she didn't say anything, and Maddie was about to retreat, thinking she had pushed too far.

Then, in a voice so quiet Maddie almost didn't hear it, Hannah whispered, "No. I'm not okay."

Maddie's heart twisted. She took a tentative step closer, her voice gentle. "Do you want to talk about it? People tell me I'm pretty good at listening."

Hannah was silent for another long moment, her shoulders rigid. Slowly, she turned around, her dark eyes glistening with unshed tears.

"I'm...pregnant," she said, her voice barely above a whisper.

Maddie's breath caught in her throat. The words hung in the air, heavy with the weight of the girl's confession. A confession Maddie wouldn't have guessed in a hundred years.

Hannah's face crumpled, and as she looked down, tears spilled onto her cheeks. "I don't know what to do," she choked out. "I don't want to tell my dad. I can't. He's barely home, and when he is, he's just angry. When he finds out about this, he will freak out."

Maddie's heart ached for the girl standing in front of her —so young, so scared, and so alone. She felt a familiar tug of grief, remembering how often she had felt lost after Jack died, not knowing where to turn or who to lean on.

Without thinking, Maddie stepped forward and gently wrapped her arms around Hannah. The girl stiffened at first, but then she crumpled into Maddie's embrace, her sobs shaking her small frame.

"It's going to be okay," Maddie whispered, stroking her hair. "You don't have to go through this alone."

For a long time, they stood there, the quiet of the house wrapping around them as Hannah cried into Maddie's shoulder. Ernie padded over, weaving between their legs as if sensing the significance of what was happening and wanting to help.

When Hannah's sobs finally subsided, Maddie pulled back slightly, holding the girl at arm's length. "We'll figure this out together, okay?"

"Why? You don't even know me."

"I know what it's like to feel alone and scared and not know what to do. And we're both women, so we've got that going for us. But mostly, you need help, and I want to do that for you."

Hannah wiped at her tear-streaked face, her eyes wide and scared. "How? What if..." A soft sob snuck out. "What if my dad kicks me out?"

Maddie's heart squeezed. "You can stay here, with Schatzi and me, as long as you need. We'll talk to your dad when you're ready, but right now, we just need to take things one step at a time. You're not alone, Hannah. I'm here. And Schatzi is here."

Maddie knew her aunt well enough to know that was true.

Hannah nodded, though the fear was still there in her eyes. But Maddie could see something else, too—something she hadn't seen before. Trust. It might be hesitant, but it was there.

And in that moment, as the fire crackled in the hearth and the snow fell softly outside, Maddie took comfort in being able to offer that to another person. To someone who was hurting in their own way.

There was something about the instant that made her think they might all be able to help each other heal.

Chapter Eleven

The air in the house felt different after Hannah's confession. The heavy burden the girl had been carrying for weeks—maybe months—hung in the corners of every room, pressing in on Maddie.

As much as she wanted to, it wasn't something she could share with Becca. It just didn't feel right, even now that they were talking again. Hannah deserved her privacy.

But as Maddie moved through the house the next day, tending to Schatzi, she couldn't stop thinking about Hannah and the sheer weight of the words she'd spoken: *I'm pregnant. I don't know what to do.*

The gravity of it all gnawed at Maddie. She had promised Hannah they'd figure it out together, but the truth was, Maddie didn't know where to begin. How could she help this girl, so young and terrified, navigate something so life-altering when Maddie herself still struggled to navigate her own grief?

Also life-altering, but not in the way bringing a child into the world was.

She stood at the kitchen sink, her hands resting on the edge of the basin over the warm dishwater, staring out the frosty window as the snow continued to flutter down. The world outside was a serene white, but inside her mind, it was anything but calm.

Ernie padded over, his soft fur brushing against Maddie's ankles as he meowed for attention. She smiled faintly, drying her hands and reaching down to scratch behind his ears. The soft purring of the cat was comforting, but her thoughts were miles away.

"How's that lunch coming along?" Schatzi's voice broke the quiet, pulling Maddie back to the present.

"It's coming," Maddie said absently, turning to glance at her aunt. Schatzi was still in her armchair, a blanket draped over her legs and her arm resting in the sling, looking more restless than usual.

Maddie left the dishes and checked on the reheating soup. It was just starting to simmer at the edges. She smiled at her aunt. "Shouldn't be but a few more minutes."

Schatzi tilted her head, her sharp blue eyes narrowing. "You've been acting strange all morning. What's on your mind? And don't say nothing because I know better."

Maddie hesitated, chewing her bottom lip as she came out to the living room. Schatzi could always read her so easily, as though her emotions were written across her face in bold letters. Maddie wasn't sure how much she should tell Schatzi about Hannah's situation, but the weight of it was too heavy to carry alone.

She had to tell Schatzi. Especially if Hannah decided she needed a place to stay.

Maddie crossed the room and sat on the edge of the sofa across from Schatzi. "It's about Hannah," she began, her voice soft but steady.

Schatzi raised her eyebrows, her lips pressing into a thin line. "Go on."

Maddie took a deep breath, folding her hands in her lap.

"She told me something yesterday. Something big and secret, but she confided in me. I'm only sharing because I know you'll keep it a secret and because I think you need to know. She's pregnant, Schatzi. And she's scared. She doesn't know how to tell her dad, and...she doesn't know what to do."

Schatzi's expression relaxed immediately, and she let out a long sigh, her eyes glazing with a mix of sadness and understanding. "Poor girl," she murmured, shaking her head slowly. "I knew something was troubling her, but I didn't think..."

"Neither did I," Maddie admitted. "She's so young, Schatzi. I don't think she even understands the enormity of what's happening. And I'm worried about her. Her dad's barely around, and when he is, she says he's angry all the time."

Schatzi was quiet briefly, her brow furrowed in thought. She shifted in her chair, grimacing slightly as she adjusted her arm in the sling. "What does she plan to do?"

Maddie shook her head, feeling the weight of the unknown settle in her chest. "She doesn't know. She hasn't even told her dad yet. I offered to let her stay here if she needs to—I hope that was okay—"

"It was fine," Schatzi reassured her.

"Good. But I'm not sure how we can help her, not really."

Schatzi's eyes softened, and she reached out with her good hand to rest it on Maddie's. "You did the right thing, Maddie. Offering her a safe place was the first step. That's what she needs most right now. Someone to show her she's not alone."

"But what about after?" Maddie asked, her voice low. "What happens if her dad can't—or won't—help her? What if she—"

"She'll have us." Schatzi's gaze held Maddie's for a long while before she spoke, her tone firm but kind. "We'll be here for her."

The certainty in Schatzi's words brought a small wave of

relief, but the enormity of the situation still loomed large. How could they take care of Hannah and the baby on top of everything else?

Most days, Maddie was barely keeping her head above water herself. Between caring for Schatzi, managing the house, doing the cooking and the laundry and trying to heal from her own grief, she felt stretched thin.

Schatzi must have sensed her worry because she squeezed Maddie's hand gently. "We'll figure it out, Maddie. One step at a time. We can't solve everything today, but we can give Hannah what she needs right now—kindness, a roof over her head, a little hope, and a safe place to land."

Maddie nodded, grateful for Schatzi's steady presence and generous heart, though her mind was still racing. Of course, they'd figure this out, but the uncertainty gnawed at her.

Just then, the sound of boots on the snow outside reached their ears, followed by a loud bark. Maddie's heart lightened as she glanced out the window to see Sam and Fargo making their way up the path, the familiar sight of the chocolate Lab bounding through the snow bringing a faint smile to her lips.

"I'll get the door," Maddie said, standing and heading toward the front entrance. The cold air hit her as she opened the door, and Fargo immediately rushed in, wagging his tail and leaving a little trail of snow as he trotted toward Schatzi's chair.

Sam followed, brushing the snow from his coat with one hand, his face bright from the cold. His other arm cradled a pile of split logs. "Afternoon," he said, his deep voice warm as he smiled at Maddie. "Brought some firewood. Thought you ladies might need it with this snow coming in."

Maddie smiled, grateful once again for his thoughtfulness. "You read our minds. We've gotten a little low. I was just thinking I should head out and get some so I didn't have to bother you."

"It's never a bother." As Sam set the firewood by the hearth, Fargo settled in front of the fire, his large body sprawling out comfortably like he was exactly where he wanted to be.

Schatzi chuckled at the dog before she looked at Sam. "You spoil us," she said to Sam, though her voice was light. "Between you and Maddie, I hardly have to lift a finger anymore."

Sam grinned, his eyes crinkling at the corners. "Good. That's the point. I'm going back out for another load. Should be enough to get you through to tomorrow."

He returned quickly, stomping his boots off on the porch as Maddie got the door. His arms were twice as full as they'd been the first time.

Maddie closed the door behind him and walked with him to the living room where she watched Sam with quiet appreciation. He had become a constant in their lives, always showing up when they needed him, always knowing just what to say to keep things from feeling too overwhelming. She found herself relying on his presence more than she cared to admit.

It had been a while since a man had had that kind of place in her life. It was a curious feeling to have one occupying it again.

As Sam stacked the firewood near the hearth, Maddie debated whether to bring up Hannah's situation. She trusted Sam, but this wasn't her secret to tell. Yet something about his calm, steady demeanor made her think he might be able to help in ways she couldn't.

"Sam," Maddie began, her voice tentative. "I need to talk to you about something...personal."

Sam paused, straightening up and brushing the wood dust from his hands. He turned to face her, his expression open but serious. "Of course. What's going on?"

Maddie took a deep breath, glancing briefly at Schatzi,

who gave her a small nod, before looking back at Sam. "It's about Hannah. She's in...a difficult situation."

Sam's brow furrowed, concern flickering in his eyes. "What kind of situation?"

"I'm not sure I should be telling you this, but I trust you. She's pregnant," Maddie said quietly, her heart squeezing as she spoke the words aloud again. "It's a secret. She hasn't told her dad yet. And you can't tell him, either."

"I won't."

"She's scared to tell him, and...she doesn't know what to do."

Sam's eyes filled with sympathy as he took in Maddie's words. He didn't speak right away, but Maddie could see the wheels turning in his mind, the concern deepening in his expression.

"That poor kid," Sam murmured, shaking his head. "No wonder she's been so withdrawn lately."

Maddie nodded. "I've offered to let her stay with us, but...I'm not sure how to help her beyond that. She's really frightened, Sam. She doesn't have much of a support system."

Sam was quiet, his gaze thoughtful as he leaned against the stone mantle. "Well, first off, you and Schatzi are doing more than enough by giving her a safe place to stay. That's huge, Maddie. She needs that stability more than anything right now."

Maddie sighed, tucking a strand of hair behind one ear. "But what about her dad? He's been distant, and she says he's angry a lot. She's worried, rightfully so, he won't take the news well."

Sam's expression darkened slightly, and he crossed his arms over his chest. "I've known Hannah's dad for a few years. Bill's a hard worker and a decent guy, but he's been through the wringer since his wife passed. Doesn't excuse his anger, though."

"Do you think he'll kick her out?" Maddie asked, her voice laced with worry.

Sam's lips pressed together, but after a second, he shook his head. "I don't think so. He might get angry, sure, but he loves Hannah. He's just lost. He's grieving, too."

Maddie nodded slowly, her thoughts spinning. It made sense—grief could warp a person, make them act in ways they normally wouldn't. She knew that all too well.

"I'll talk to him," Sam offered, his voice steady. "When Hannah's ready, I'll be there to help break the news. We'll figure it out. You're not in this alone."

Maddie blinked, her heart swelling with gratitude. Sam had a way of easing her burdens without making her feel like she was asking too much. "Thank you," she whispered. "I didn't want to ask, but I knew you could help, and I was right."

Sam smiled gently, his eyes full of warmth. "You don't have to ask. That's what neighbors, and friends, do."

As the fire crackled and the snow continued to fall outside, Maddie felt a small spark of happiness ignite in her chest. Friends. That was nice.

Maybe, with Sam's help, they could give Hannah the support she needed. And maybe they could all navigate this new ground together, as a sort of community.

It was a comforting thought. For the first time since Hannah had shared her news, Maddie felt like things were going to be okay.

Chapter Twelve

The next few days passed in a quiet blur, the snow outside piling higher as the mountain became an isolated world of its own. Inside Aunt Schatzi's cozy house, Maddie tried to keep things as normal as possible, though her mind was constantly occupied with thoughts of Hannah and the difficult conversations that had yet to happen.

When the girl came by to clean, Maddie watched her move through the house with heavy steps, the weight of her secret still hanging over her. It only increased Maddie's desire to help, but just like Hannah's last visit, the girl was in no mood to talk.

Schatzi was resting more, as the sling kept her movements limited, and she spent most of her time sitting by the fire reading books or watching television, Ernie snuggled up beside her. Maddie could sense Schatzi's worry for Hannah too, though they hadn't spoken much more about it. The quiet hum of shared concerns and unspoken words was a constant presence in the house.

One afternoon, as Maddie stood in the kitchen making

sandwiches for lunch, there was a knock at the door. Startled, she jumped—Hannah wasn't due to come by until later in the week, so she knew it must be Sam. He had been stopping by more frequently, checking in, and though Maddie was growing accustomed to his presence, every visit brought a new mix of relief and nerves.

As she'd expected, Maddie opened the door to find Sam standing there, his brown eyes warm despite the biting cold. Fargo, as usual, stood beside him, his tail wagging, the dog always happy to be included.. He barked softly in greeting.

"Hi, Fargo. Hi, Sam."

"Afternoon," Sam said, stepping inside as the cold air followed him. "Thought I'd drop by and see how things are going. Check if you needed anything."

Maddie smiled, though it didn't quite feel it. "Thanks. Come in. I was just making some sandwiches for lunch."

"Afternoon, Sam," Schatzi called out from her chair.

"Afternoon, Schatzi." Sam kicked the snow from his boots before coming in, then hung his coat on a peg by the door, the familiar scent of cold air and pine clinging to him. He lowered his voice when he spoke to Maddie next. "How's she doing today?"

"She's getting better, though I can tell she's frustrated with the sling," Maddie replied, leading him into the kitchen. "She hates sitting still for too long but the best she can do is take a few laps around the living room when she gets antsy. Which is often."

Sam chuckled, leaning against the counter as Fargo went into the living room and made himself comfortable on the rug by the fire. "That sounds like Schatzi."

Maddie busied herself fixing the rest of the sandwiches, trying to ignore the way her stomach fluttered in Sam's presence. He was so steady, so easy to be around, but every time he was close, something inside her shifted, like an old door creaking open after being shut for years. She wasn't ready to face what that meant just yet.

"Any updates on how Hannah's doing?" Sam asked after a beat, his voice lowering further. "I haven't seen her dad lately. Guess he's trying to work as many hours as he can before the holidays."

Maddie hesitated, her hand stilling as she spread mayonnaise on the bread with a knife.. "She's still scared. She hasn't told her dad yet. I don't want to push her, but I don't know how long she can keep this a secret. Eventually, it's going to come out."

Sam crossed his arms, his brow furrowing in thought. "Have you talked to her about it again? About telling him?"

"I've tried," Maddie said, setting the knife down and turning to face him. "She clams up every time I bring it up. Like maybe she regrets telling me. I don't want to scare her off by pushing too hard, but we can't avoid this forever. She certainly can't."

Sam nodded, his face softening with understanding. "It's tough. But you're right. She can't keep it a secret forever. Even if this wasn't a small town, it's the kind of thing that becomes impossible to ignore at a certain point."

Maddie sighed, leaning against the counter. "I know. But she's just so afraid. I don't want to make it harder for her than it already is."

Sam stepped closer, his voice gentle. "You're doing the right thing, Maddie. She needs to tell him, but she also needs to know she's got people behind her, no matter what happens. Which I think she does."

"I hope so, but maybe I should remind her." Maddie looked up at him, her heart swelling with gratitude. He had been such a steady presence through all of this, and she didn't know how she would have managed without him. "Thanks, Sam. I really appreciate you being here."

He smiled the kind of smile that made the room feel a little warmer. "Anytime."

Later that afternoon, as the sun beamed bright over the snowy landscape, the knock on the door that Maddie had been dreading finally came. She finished filling the kettle and set it on a burner to heat before going to the door. This time, it *was* Hannah.

The girl stood in the entrance, bundled up in her oversized coat, her dark hair tucked under a knit hat. Her face was pale, and there was a tension in her posture that made Maddie's heart ache.

"Hi, Hannah," Maddie said, stepping aside to let her in. "Come on in. It's freezing out there."

Hannah shuffled inside, her boots leaving wet tracks on the floor as she moved to take off her coat. Maddie watched her, trying to gauge how she was feeling, but the girl's expression was unreadable.

"How are you doing?" Maddie asked, closing the door behind her.

Hannah shrugged, her eyes fixed on the floor. "Okay, I guess."

Maddie didn't press further, knowing the conversation ahead would be delicate. She led Hannah into the living room, where Schatzi greeted her warmly from her armchair. Ernie was stretched out beside her, purring softly and no doubt enjoying the warmth of the fire.

"Good to see you, Hannah," Schatzi said, her voice kind. "You're just in time. Maddie's making tea. You want some?"

Hannah nodded mutely, taking a seat on the sofa. Her hands fidgeted in her lap, twisting the edge of her sweater as though she were trying to keep herself from unraveling.

Right on cue, the kettle whistled. Maddie went into the kitchen, fixed three mugs of tea, and brought them back. They all sat and drank, and Maddie could feel the tension radiating off of Hannah. After a few minutes of small-talk, Maddie decided it was time to tackle the elephant in the room.

She was already seated next to Hannah, so she cleared her throat slightly and began. "Hannah, Schatzi and I want to talk about what we discussed the other week."

Hannah's shoulders tensed, and she stared into her tea, her jaw tight, her hands clenched around the mug. "I don't want to."

"I know it's hard," Maddie said gently, "but we can't avoid this. You need to tell your dad."

Hannah set her cup on the side table and shook her head, her hands balling into fists in her lap. "He's going to freak out. He'll...he'll kick me out, I know it."

Maddie's heart clenched at the fear in Hannah's voice. "You don't know that for sure," she said. "And if he does, you have a place here. I promise you that."

"We both do," Schatzi said. "You'll never be without a home."

"You don't get it." Hannah blinked back tears, her eyes wide and filled with desperation. "I don't want him to hate me. He's the only parent I have left."

The sheer pain in her voice made Maddie's chest tighten. She reached out to take Hannah's hand. "He won't hate you, Hannah. He loves you. He might be upset at first, but he'll come around. Maybe it'll take time, but he will. And even if he doesn't handle it well initially, you'll get through this. We'll get through this together. You are *not* going to be alone."

Hannah's lips trembled, and for a moment, Maddie thought she was going to break down again. But then she nodded, a tiny, hesitant nod that gave Maddie hope.

"Okay. I'll tell him," Hannah whispered, her voice barely audible. "But I can't do it alone."

"You won't have to," Maddie said firmly, giving her hand a

little squeeze. "Sam and I will be there with you when you tell him. If you want us to be."

Hannah looked up, her eyes glistening with a mix of fear and gratitude. "You will? Both of you?"

"Of course," Maddie replied, her voice steady. "We'll go with you, and we'll help you explain everything. We'll be right by your side."

Schatzi, who had been listening quietly from her chair, gave a nod of approval. "You've got more people looking out for you than you realize, Hannah."

Hannah wiped at her eyes, sniffling as she managed a small, shaky smile. It only lasted a second, but it had been there. "Thank you."

A day later, Maddie, Sam, and Hannah stood on the snowy front steps of Hannah's house, the tension between them almost unbearable. The house was small and weathered, a stark contrast to the snowy beauty surrounding it.

Maddie's breath formed clouds in the icy air, and her heart thumped as they stood in silence, waiting for Hannah's father to open the door. She prayed this went well. Or at least better than Hannah was anticipating.

Sam stood beside Hannah, his imposing figure offering quiet strength. Hannah had asked that he be there for the conversation, and Maddie was grateful for his steady presence. She could feel Hannah's nervousness, and she gently placed a hand on the girl's arm in support.

The door opened with a creak, and a middle-aged man stood in the doorway, his face haggard and drawn, the stubble on his cheeks a few days old. Maddie didn't know the man, but she immediately knew that grief had carved itself into his features. His eyes were tired, and his expression grew wary as he took in the sight of Hannah standing with Maddie and Sam.

"Dad," Hannah said, her voice shaking. "Can we talk?"

Her father's brow furrowed, his gaze moving between the three of them. "What's going on?" he asked, his voice gruff but not unkind.

"I just want to talk to you," Hannah said.

"About what? Why do you need these folks?"

Hannah swallowed hard, and for a second, it looked like she might retreat, like she might run from this unwelcome confrontation. But then she squared her shoulders and lifted her chin, her voice small but determined. "Because they're here to support me. I'm sorry, it wasn't planned, but...I'm pregnant."

The words hung in the cold air, freezing everything in place. Maddie held her breath, her pulse pounding in her ears as she waited for the man's reaction.

Silence spooled out, thick and uncomfortable. Hannah's father stood frozen in the doorway, his face unreadable. Then, slowly, his expression shifted—first to confusion, then to disbelief, and finally to anger.

"You're *what*?" he said, his voice rising with shock. "Pregnant? Hannah, how could you—"

"Please," Maddie interjected gently, stepping forward. "Let's sit down and talk about this. It's taken a lot of courage for Hannah to get here."

Hannah's father looked at Maddie, his eyes wide with fury. "You knew? An adult? And you didn't think you should tell me?"

Maddie kept her voice calm. "It's her information to share and she needed time, plus, she was scared. We're only here to support and help in whatever way we can, I give you my word."

Sam nodded. "She's right, Bill."

Bill's chest heaved as he stared at his daughter, his emotions clearly a whirlwind of anger and hurt. "Scared? What about me? How am I supposed to deal with this?"

"She's *your* daughter," Sam said, his voice low and firm. "She needs your support now more than ever. Let us come in and sit down so we can discuss this."

Hannah's father seemed frozen in place. Only his face twisted with emotion, and Maddie could see the battle waging inside him. But then, slowly, his shoulders slumped, and he let out a shaky breath.

"Come inside then," he muttered, stepping back from the door. "So we can...talk."

As they stepped into the warmth of the house, Maddie felt a surge of relief. It wasn't going to be easy, but they had made it through the hardest part. Hannah's news was no longer a secret.

Hannah squeezed Maddie's hand and, for the first time in days, Maddie saw a flicker of hope in the girl's eyes.

As they sat down around the small, worn kitchen table, Maddie knew it would take some doing, but they would get through this together, one step at a time. She'd promised Hannah she would be here to support her in whatever way she needed, and Maddie still meant that.

No matter what Hannah's father ultimately decided, Hannah and her baby would not be alone in this.

Chapter Thirteen

Tension thickened the air in Bill's small house as they all sat at the kitchen table. The faint ticking of the wall clock was the only sound that filled the silence, amplifying the nervous energy that hummed between them.

Bill, visibly shaken, sat across from them, his gaze traveling back and forth from his daughter to Maddie and Sam, as if trying to make sense of everything. He looked tired and worn down, the same way Maddie had felt right after losing Jack.

Finding out his daughter was pregnant couldn't be easy, not on top of everything else he had to deal with.

But Maddie's heart ached for Hannah the most. She was the one who had to bear the heaviest burden.

The girl sat stiffly, hands clasped tightly in her lap, her eyes downcast. The quiet girl Maddie had come to know, who had been holding onto this secret for so long, now seemed smaller than ever. Vulnerable. Maddie could sense the fear radiating off her in waves, and it made Maddie want to reach across the table and shield her from the storm she knew was brewing.

Hannah's father cleared his throat, the sound rough and strained, breaking the uncomfortable silence. His face had gone nearly colorless, and the furrows in his brow seemed deeper than ever.

"I—I don't understand," he said, his voice hoarse. He looked directly at Hannah for the first time since she'd broken the news. "How could this happen? I didn't even know you were seeing anyone."

Hannah didn't lift her eyes from the table, her fingers twisting in her lap as though she was trying to disappear into herself.

"It...it wasn't supposed to happen," Hannah murmured, her voice barely above a whisper. "It was an accident."

"Who is he?"

Hannah gave a little shake of her head. "He's not in the picture anymore and that's how I want it to stay. I swear, Dad, it was just a mistake."

Her father's jaw tightened, his hands curling into fists on the table. Maddie could see the struggle in his eyes—the anger warring with the heartbreak. He let out a ragged breath, shaking his head.

"A mistake," he repeated, his voice raw with disbelief. "This...this is more than a mistake, Hannah. This changes everything. This is not the future I wanted for you. And certainly not the one your mom wanted for you."

"I know," Hannah whispered, tears brimming in her eyes. "I'm sorry, Dad. I didn't mean for this to happen."

Maddie's heart clenched as she watched the way Hannah's father's words pressed down on her already burdened shoulders. Maddie wanted to speak, to say something to ease the tension, but she knew this was a conversation Hannah needed to have with her father. Just like she needed to face the truth of her situation, as painful as it was.

Sam, ever steady, leaned forward slightly, his voice calm but firm. "She didn't want to hide it from you, Bill. She deserves some credit for that. She's scared, but she's trying to take responsibility."

Hannah's father looked up at Sam, his eyes filled with a mix of anger and frustration. "Great, but how am I supposed to take this? My sixteen-year-old daughter is pregnant. I—" His voice broke, and he looked back at Hannah, his expression softening ever so slightly. "You're just a kid."

Hannah sniffled, finally lifting her gaze to meet his. "I'm not a kid anymore, Dad. I know that now."

The raw honesty in her voice hung between them like a lifeline, pulling her father back from the edge of his anger. His shoulders sagged in resignation, the fire in his eyes dimming as he let out a long, heavy sigh. He swallowed twice before speaking again.

"I don't know how we're going to handle this," he said, more to himself than to anyone else. "But we're going to have to figure it out."

Hannah blinked, clearly not expecting those words, and the hope that flickered in her eyes was like a spark in the darkness. "You mean...you don't hate me?"

Her father's face crumpled and he shook his head, running a hand through his graying hair. "Hannah, I could never hate you. I'm angry and I'm scared and I'm worried. But hate doesn't even enter the picture. You're my daughter, and that doesn't change because of this. Nothing changes that. I love you. Always will."

The tension in the room seemed to release all at once, and Maddie felt her own breath return. Things weren't perfect—there was so much they had to work through—but this was a start. The hardest part was over now. Hannah had told him, and they could move forward, figure out a plan.

Hannah wiped her eyes, a shaky smile forming on her lips. "Thanks, Dad. I love you, too. Does that mean you're not going to kick me out?"

"No, sweetheart. I am not going to kick you out." Her father reached across the table, his hand trembling slightly as he took hers. The gesture was small, but it was enough to tell Maddie that they had made it through the worst of the storm.

The walk back to Schatzi's house was quiet, but there was a palpable shift in the air, as if some of the weight that had been pressing down on them had finally lifted. All of their moods were vastly improved. Hannah had come with them to get her things. She'd dropped a bag off earlier, in case the talk with her dad didn't go well.

The snow had begun to fall again, soft flakes drifting lazily through the air, and the world around them was still and serene, as if it, too, had been waiting for this moment of calm.

Hannah walked between Maddie and Sam, her head down but her steps lighter. Maddie could sense the relief radiating off of her, though the girl hadn't said much since they'd left the house.

"You did great today, Hannah," Sam said softly, breaking the silence. "That wasn't easy. You did some real character building in there."

Hannah glanced up at him, her eyes red-rimmed but filled with gratitude. "Thank you. I don't think I could've done it without you guys beside me."

Maddie smiled, warmth spreading through her. "You're tougher than you think, Hannah. You handled it with more grace and maturity than I ever could have at your age."

Hannah shrugged, her shoulders tense, but there was a small smile tugging at the corner of her lips. "I don't feel tough. I feel scared. And a little stupid."

"You're not stupid just because this happened. Life throws us curveballs all the time. As for the scared part? That's normal," Maddie said gently. "But you've taken the hardest step. You told him. You got through that. Now, you can focus on what's next. And we'll help you every step of the way."

Hannah's gaze softened, and for the first time since Maddie had met her, there was a glimmer of peace in her eyes. She nodded, her steps slowing as they reached the edge of Schatzi's front yard.

The house looked warm and inviting against the backdrop of the snowy mountains, smoke curling from the chimney and the soft glow of the firelight spilling through the windows. Maddie smiled as they approached the front door, grateful for the sense of safety and comfort the house provided.

"I should get my stuff and get going," Hannah said quietly, stopping just outside the door. "I don't want to impose..."

"You're not imposing," Maddie said firmly. "You're always welcome here, Hannah. Come in for a few minutes. I'm sure Schatzi would love to see you and know that everything's all right."

Hannah hesitated, glancing between Maddie and Sam before nodding. "Okay. Just for a little while."

Maddie opened the door, the warmth from inside rushing out to greet them as they stepped into the cozy living room. Schatzi was sitting in her armchair, Ernie curled up on her lap, but she looked up and smiled brightly when she saw them.

"Well, look who it is!" Schatzi exclaimed, her eyes twinkling as she spotted Hannah. "I was wondering when I'd see you again, young lady. Come on in, sit by the fire. You look half-frozen."

Hannah smiled shyly and took off her coat, hanging it by the door before sitting on the sofa across from Schatzi. The fire crackled softly in the hearth, filling the room with a comforting warmth, and Maddie felt a sense of calm settle over her. The house was alive with the kind of warmth that wasn't just from the fire—it was the warmth of connection, of family.

"How did things go?" Schatzi asked.

"They went all right," Hannah answered. "Better than I thought they would."

"That's wonderful news."

"How are you feeling, Schatzi?" Sam asked, leaning against the wall as Fargo, who'd stayed with Schatzi, trotted over to sit at Sam's feet.

"Oh, you know me," Schatzi said with a dramatic sigh. "I'm just sitting here, trying not to let this sling get the best of me. I'm not used to being fussed over so much." She gave Maddie a teasing glance, though her smile was full of affection.

Maddie chuckled and shook her head. "Well, you're stuck with me for now. So you'll have to get used to it."

Schatzi waved her hand dismissively, but her eyes softened as she looked around the room, taking in the sight of Maddie, Hannah, and Sam all together. "I suppose there are worse things than being surrounded by good company."

Hannah smiled, but there was still a hint of uncertainty in her eyes. Maddie noticed it, but before she could say anything, Schatzi leaned forward in her chair, her voice lowering.

"You'll be all right, you know," Schatzi said, her gaze locked on Hannah. "I don't need to know all the details of what happened with your dad, but I already know you're going to be okay. And I'll tell you something I've learned from living in these mountains all these years: life gives us hard things, but that's just to teach us how strong we are. You can do this."

Hannah's eyes glistened with unshed tears, and she nodded, her voice barely above a whisper as she said, "Thank you, Schatzi."

Maddie's heart swelled with warmth, the tension of the day easing as she watched Hannah relax in the comfort of

Schatzi's words. It wasn't going to be easy for any of them—there were still challenges ahead, still fears to face—but to Maddie it felt like they were finally on the right path.

As the fire crackled and the snow continued to fall outside, Maddie glanced at Sam, who caught her eye and gave her a small, reassuring smile. There was something unspoken between them, a quiet understanding that they were in this together. Not just for Hannah, but for a bigger purpose. That of bringing new life safely into the world.

The weight of grief that had once felt so crushing now felt lighter, like it was something manageable that Maddie could carry with her, instead of something that held her back. The warmth of the house, the people in it, had melted away the protective ice that had surrounded her heart for so long.

Having other people to care about was definitely helping, too. It forced her to turn her focus outward instead of inward, as it had been since Jack had passed.

And as she sat there, surrounded by the quiet hum of companionship and the soft flicker of the firelight, Maddie realized that she was no longer just surviving day to day.

She was starting to live again.

Chapter Fourteen

The day of Christmas Eve arrived quietly, blanketing the mountain house in a stillness that felt both peaceful and heavy. Snow had once again fallen through the night, covering the yard in a thick white layer.

Maddie and Schatzi had both gotten up late, had a simple breakfast of cinnamon toast, and spent most of the day watching old Christmas movies. Lunch had been soup left over from the day before. Keeping things easy seemed to be the theme of the day.

Now the light was starting to fade outside. A cup of tea in hand, Maddie found herself standing at the kitchen window, watching the flakes continue to drift down. The world outside looked untouched, serene, as if it had paused to allow the holiday to settle in gently.

Inside, the warmth of the house was steady and comforting, though there was a tension in the air that hadn't been there before. Maddie could feel it—something unresolved, like unfinished business hanging over the festive mood. Despite the crackling fire and the smell of pine from the small

Christmas tree she'd set up in the corner, there was a sense of anticipation.

Maddie wasn't sure what they were waiting for. Perhaps it was the fact that, for her, this was another Christmas without Jack—or maybe it was the lingering worries about Hannah's future. Regardless, Maddie couldn't shake the feeling that tonight would be important, a turning point for all of them.

She turned away from the window and busied herself in the kitchen, preparing the Christmas Eve dinner she and Schatzi had planned earlier in the week. It was nothing too over the top—a small turkey to roast, green beans, mashed potatoes and gravy, sweet potato biscuits—just the usual Christmas fare.

But it was enough to make the house smell like home. Maddie hummed softly to herself as she did the prep of peeling potatoes, the rhythm of the task calming her nerves.

In the living room, Schatzi sat in her usual chair, her knitting needles clicking softly as she worked on a scarf for Hannah.

Despite the sling, Schatzi had insisted on taking up her knitting again. She said it was her way of keeping her hands busy, of doing something productive while she recovered. Maddie had given up trying to stop her.

Hannah had come over early to see if there was anything that needed doing. There hadn't been, so now she sat on the sofa, curled up with a blanket and a mug of tea. She had been coming over more frequently, finding solace in the warmth of Schatzi's house, though she still hadn't said much about what was going on with her father.

Maddie knew the situation wasn't fully resolved. According to Sam, who was outside getting firewood, Hannah's father had been quiet since their conversation, processing everything in his own time. Maddie was just grateful that he hadn't kicked Hannah out or refused to speak to her.

Fargo lay at Hannah's feet, his brown fur a comforting presence as he snored faintly, oblivious to the tension in the room. Maddie smiled at the sight of him, thankful for the quiet companionship he provided. Sam had come for dinner but arrived early to see what needed to be done. He'd brought a delicious-looking pumpkin roll as his contribution, bought from a great little bakery in town.

As if he needed to contribute anything. He'd already shoveled the walkways and made a path to the mailbox. Just his presence brought Maddie a sense of relief. His steadfastness had become something she looked forward to more than she was willing to admit.

The door creaked open, letting in a gust of cold air, and Maddie turned to see Sam stepping inside, a dusting of snow on his coat and hat. His cheeks were pink from the cold, and he carried a load of firewood in one arm.

"Hey," he said, his voice warm as he stepped out of his boots. "Got some wood but might bring some more in, in case this storm keeps up through the night."

"Thanks, Sam," Maddie said, smiling as she wiped her hands on a towel. "I think we'll be set for the whole winter at this rate."

He chuckled, setting the firewood down by the hearth, then going outside for one more bundle. When that was taken care of, he hung up his coat and came to sit in the other chair near the fire.

Fargo immediately perked up, trotting over to greet Sam with a wagging tail and a happy bark. Sam gave the dog a good scratch behind the ears, then turned to Schatzi and Hannah, his smile bright.

"How's everyone holding up?" he asked, his gaze lingering on Hannah.

Schatzi shrugged her good shoulder. "Oh, you know me. Just sitting here pretending I have a perfectly good arm underneath this blasted sling."

Maddie smiled, but her attention was on Hannah, who had pulled the blanket tighter around her shoulders. The girl had been quieter than usual all day, her mood subdued despite the holiday. Maddie wondered if she was thinking about her mother because the holiday had brought back so many memories that were too hard to face. That was something Maddie could certainly understand.

"I'm fine," Hannah murmured, though her eyes were downcast. "Just...thinking, you know?"

Sam glanced at Maddie, who gave him a small nod of understanding. They both knew Hannah was still struggling, but neither wanted to make her talk about it if she wasn't ready. It seemed like the best thing they could offer her was space. And the understanding that she wasn't alone.

"Well," Sam said, "if you ever need to talk, you know we're here to listen. And where to find us."

Hannah nodded, her expression remained tense, and Maddie could see the weight of everything she'd been carrying. It wasn't fair, she thought, that someone so young had to bear so much.

There was a little small-talk during dinner, and lots of compliments on the food, but otherwise, it was pretty quiet, the clink of forks against plates filling the silence between bites. Maddie had worked hard to make the meal feel special, but it was clear that everyone was caught up in their own thoughts. She'd be lying if she said that wasn't a disappointment, but what could she do? She didn't want to say anything. That wasn't going to help.

Even Schatzi, usually so full of energy and quips, seemed quieter tonight, her gaze drifting to Hannah every now and then as if trying to gauge how the girl was feeling.

Sam sat across from Maddie, his presence as welcome as always, although he, too, seemed preoccupied. Maddie couldn't help but notice the way his gaze occasionally wandered in her direction with a certain thoughtfulness, as though he were trying to figure out what was going on in her head.

She wondered if he could sense her unease—if he knew that tonight, of all nights, felt weighted by memories in a way she hadn't expected.

As they finished dinner and moved to the living room for dessert, the fire crackled warmly in the hearth, casting a soft glow over the room. Despite having one arm in a sling, Schatzi, always determined to make Christmas special, had pulled out a few decorations from the attic earlier in the week. Though they were sparse, the small tree in the corner sparkled with twinkling lights, a few red and gold balls, and a small gold star on top.

Schatzi settled into her chair, moving Ernie over enough to make room for herself. He looked a little put out, but went back to sleep after a second.

Maddie sliced up the pumpkin roll and plated it. With Hannah's help, they handed out the dessert and mugs of hot chocolate garnished with little marshmallows as they all sat down by the fire. For a few moments, the quiet warmth of the room soothed the tension she'd been feeling all day.

They ate their dessert, which was the perfect combination of pumpkin and cake with plenty of whipped filling, and watched the fire. When they were done, Maddie gathered up the plates and took them into the kitchen.

As she sat back down, Hannah spoke, her voice barely above a whisper. "I miss her," she said, staring into her mug, her voice trembling. "I miss my mom."

The room went still. Maddie's heart clamped down, the ache so familiar, and she could see Schatzi shift in her chair, her eyes going tender with sympathy. Sam remained quiet, his gaze steady on Hannah.

"I know," Schatzi said softly, her gaze focused on the fire, her words framed with understanding. "I miss her too."

Hannah blinked, her eyes filling with tears as she looked up at Schatzi, her lip trembling. "It just doesn't feel right. Christmas, I mean. It's not the same without her."

Maddie's throat tightened, and she set her mug down on the coffee table, moving to sit closer to Hannah on the sofa. She didn't say anything at first, just wrapped her arms around the girl and pulled her into a hug.

Hannah stiffened briefly, as if surprised by the gesture, then she melted into Maddie's embrace, her body shaking with quiet sobs.

"I know, sweetheart," Maddie whispered, stroking her hair gently. "I know it doesn't feel the same. But you're not alone. We're all here with you. And your mom is here in spirit, I know she is."

Hannah nodded, burying her face in Maddie's shoulder as she cried softly. Schatzi watched from her chair, her own eyes glistening with unshed tears, and even Sam looked affected by the raw emotion in the room. He sat quietly, his eyes never leaving Hannah as she released the pain she had been holding in for so long.

Fargo, sensitive in that way only dogs knew how to be, came over and laid his head on Hannah's knees.

In typical cat form, Ernie stayed curled up against Schatzi leg, indifferent to everything going on around him.

After a while, Hannah's sobs quieted, and she pulled back from Maddie, wiping at her eyes with the sleeve of her sweater. "I'm sorry," she murmured, her voice thick with emotion. "I didn't mean to ruin Christmas."

"Don't be silly. You didn't ruin anything," Schatzi said firmly, her voice filled with love and a tiny bit of amusement.

"This is part of Christmas too. A big part. Remembering. Grieving. Reminiscing. Storytelling. Those are all things we do around certain dates that bring to mind all the loved ones who've gone before us. It's part of life. It's part of being human."

Hannah sniffled, nodding as she glanced around the room. The fire crackled softly in the hearth, the tree lights twinkling in the corner, and for the first time that night, a small smile tugged at her lips.

"I just...wish she were here," Hannah whispered.

"I know," Maddie said quietly. "But I think, in a way, she is. She's with you, Hannah. In your memories. In the way you think of her. That doesn't go away. Just like how she's a part of you. And a part of that baby you're carrying."

Hannah looked at Maddie, her eyes still watery but filled with something Maddie hadn't seen before—acceptance. It wasn't perfect, and the pain would never fully leave, but Maddie could see that Hannah was beginning to understand that grief didn't mean the end of everything. It was something they all carried, but it didn't have to keep them from living.

Schatzi broke the heavy silence with a small, warm smile. "Well, now that we've had a good cry, who's up for some Christmas carols?"

Hannah let out a light, watery laugh, shaking her head. "I don't think I can sing right now."

"That's all right," Schatzi said with a wink. "I'll sing enough for both of us."

Maddie smiled, her heart swelling with warmth as Schatzi began with *Silent Night*, her voice soft but steady. Maddie picked up the tune, and Sam surprised her by joining in, his deep voice adding a comforting layer to the melody, and soon, the room was filled with the quiet sound of voices raised in song.

Maddie leaned back against the sofa, her arm still around

Hannah's shoulders, and for the first time since the day had begun, she felt the tension leave her body. The evening had been hard, harder than she had anticipated, but as she sat there, surrounded by people who cared for one another, she realized that it hadn't been a bad night after all.

It had been real, raw, and filled with the kind of love that could only come from facing the hardest truths together. They were blessed to have Schatzi's years of wisdom and experience.

And as the snow continued to drift down outside, Schatzi began to tell a story about Sherryl, Hannah's mother, a funny tale about a bingo night at the church hall that soon had them all laughing.

Sam chimed in with how Sherryl used to make him his favorite butterscotch chip cookies on his birthday, which got another story out of Schatzi, this time about how Sherryl had organized a bachelor auction to raise money for the firehouse.

Laughing at Schatzi's retelling, Maddie knew that this Christmas, though different from any she'd ever known, was exactly what she needed.

Chapter Fifteen

C hristmas morning dawned quietly over the mountains, the sun's pink glow spreading across the snow-covered landscape. Maddie woke early, the house still and silent around her. Not quite ready to get up, she stayed in bed beneath the heavy quilt. She felt a sense of peace, a fragile but welcome feeling.

She got up and dressed in a warm sweater and leggings before peeking through the windows. Outside, the world seemed untouched, the snow glittering under the pale winter sun, and a feeling filled her that seemed very much like hope.

She hadn't expected this Christmas to be anything special. Not after everything she'd been through. They'd already agreed that being together was the only gift any of them needed.

But last night, sitting around the fire with Hannah, Schatzi, and Sam, had changed something in her. They had shared so many wonderful stories. Some funny, some sweet, some deeply moving. It had been good for her soul in a lot of ways.

In that moment, Maddie had realized that the life she had

been trying so hard to avoid was still happening—still filled with connection and meaning, even in the midst of loss. Life no longer felt so much like something to be endured, but something to be enjoyed.

Something to be anticipated. And wasn't that a new feeling?

She stretched, breathing in the faint smell of pine and wood smoke that lingered in the air, and smiled to herself. She had survived Christmas Eve. And now, maybe she could begin to look forward to what came next.

Pulling on thick socks, Maddie padded down the stairs toward the living room. The house was quiet, the glow of the tree lights casting gentle shadows across the floor. Schatzi, and Hannah, who'd slept over, were still in their beds, and Maddie cherished the quiet of the early morning. Ernie wasn't around, no doubt curled up on Schatzi's bed. Once she got up, he'd come down with her to bask in the warmth of the fire.

Which meant Maddie had better make sure there was a fire. She add a few logs to it and poked at the embers to bring them to life. With that done, she moved toward the window and pulled back the curtain slightly, looking out at the snow-draped landscape. It was a Christmas card come to life. The trees heavy with snow, the mountains in the distance wrapped in a wintry haze. The sky was clear and blue, the sunlight gentle as it filtered through the trees.

She'd call Becca today and wish her sister and her family a merry Christmas.

As she turned back to the kitchen, intending to make a pot of coffee before everyone else woke up, there was a knock at the door. The sound startled her—it was early, and she hadn't expected anyone to be out on this cold Christmas morning. Or arriving at Schatzi's, for that matter.

Frowning slightly, she crossed the living room and opened the door to find a young woman standing on the porch, bundled in a thick coat and scarf, her cheeks flushed from the cold. Maddie's breath caught in her throat. She thought she recognized the woman, maybe from the bonfire, though she couldn't place her name.

"Hannah's not in trouble, is she?" The woman's voice was low, rushed, her eyes filled with worry. "I heard—"

"What? Hannah?" Maddie blinked in confusion, her hand still on the door. "No, she's fine. Who are you?"

The young woman's face softened, and she let out a small sigh of relief. "I'm sorry...I didn't mean to show up like this. My name's Lisa. I...I'm Trevor's—the baby's father's—sister."

The words hung in the brisk morning air, the weight of them crashing down on Maddie. The father's sister? She hadn't expected anyone connected to the baby's father to appear so suddenly. Especially not today of all days.

Lisa's dark eyes searched Maddie's face, as if she were trying to figure out how much she knew. "I just found out yesterday," Lisa said quietly, her breath forming small clouds in the cold. "About Hannah and the baby. As far as I know, my brother doesn't have a clue. Yet. I'm sure that will change, but I don't think he'll care. Anyway, I thought she might need someone."

Maddie's mind spun. She had never asked Hannah for details about the baby's father—she hadn't wanted to press her for information she didn't seem comfortable sharing. But now, standing here on the porch with Lisa, Maddie realized that this was a part of the situation they hadn't accounted for.

And there was no avoiding it now.

"Come inside," Maddie said, stepping back to let her in. "It's freezing out here."

Lisa hesitated, then nodded and stepped into the warmth of the house, her boots leaving small clumps of snow on the floor. She looked around, taking in the cozy living room, the little Christmas tree, and the crackling fire.

"Maybe I shouldn't have come," Lisa admitted, unwrapping her scarf and shrugging off her coat. "But I heard that Hannah was pregnant, and I couldn't just...do nothing. My brother—well, I love him, but he doesn't exactly have the best track record with responsibility."

Maddie raised an eyebrow as she took Lisa's coat and hung it on the peg by the door. "I see. You *heard* Hannah was pregnant? Did she tell you?" Hannah had never mentioned talking to Lisa. Or even knowing her.

Lisa shook her head. "No. I overheard a conversation in town, and I figured it out." She glanced toward the stairs, her expression softening. "I didn't want to make things harder for her. I just thought she might need help. I swear that's the only reason I'm here. That's my niece or nephew she's carrying. I owe her any help I can give."

"That's very kind of you." Maddie took a deep breath, her mind whirling as she tried to figure out what more to say. This was uncharted territory for all of them—especially for Hannah, who had been trying so hard to keep things quiet until she could figure out exactly what she was going to do. Lisa's arrival made things even more complicated.

"Hannah's been through a lot," Maddie said with care, twisting her hands together. "She's scared. But she's strong, and she's trying to make the best decisions she can. She's been hanging out here a lot, even staying over some nights, because she and her dad are struggling a bit."

Lisa nodded, her eyes filled with a kind of quiet understanding. "I get that. I do. I don't want to cause any more trouble for her. I just want to help, if I can. If she wants my help. She might not and if that's the case, I'll accept that."

Maddie hesitated, then nodded slowly. "Maybe it would be best if we talked to her together. But I should tell you she might not want to talk. This has been a lot for her to handle, and she might not be ready to take on any more."

Lisa bit her lip, glancing down at her hands. "Yeah. I figured she might not want to see me, but I thought I'd try."

Maddie gave her a small, reassuring smile. "Let's give her a minute to wake up, and then we'll talk to her. In the meantime, why don't you sit by the fire. I'll make us some coffee."

Lisa nodded gratefully, moving toward the living room as Maddie headed into the kitchen. Her mind buzzed with everything that had just happened—the sudden appearance of Lisa, the fact that someone in town was already talking about Hannah's pregnancy, and the realization that they had reached a turning point in this journey.

There was no going back. Maddie hoped Hannah would be able to handle whatever came next.

It wasn't long before Schatzi shuffled down the stairs, her steps slow and deliberate as she adjusted her sling. Ernie plodded alongside her, not moving much faster. Maddie smiled at her aunt, pouring two mugs of coffee and handing one to Schatzi as she headed for her chair by the fire.

Schatzi took a sip, her eyes narrowing as she saw Lisa sitting quietly on the sofa. "And who's this, then?"

Maddie took a breath, bracing herself for the explanation. "This is Lisa. She's the sister of the baby's father, Trevor."

Schatzi's eyebrows shot up, and she glanced sharply at Maddie before looking back at Lisa. "I see."

"Lisa, this is my aunt, Schatzi. This is her house."

Lisa shifted nervously in her seat, her hands clasped around her mug of coffee. "I didn't mean to intrude. I just wanted to offer my help. If Hannah is interested."

Schatzi, always quick to assess people, studied Lisa before her expression eased. "Well, if you're here to help, then I reckon that's a good thing. Poor Hannah's been carrying too much on her own."

Lisa nodded, though she still looked nervous. "That's what I figured."

"But if she doesn't want to talk to you—"

"I won't force myself on her, I promise."

"Good."

As the three of them sat quietly, sipping coffee and waiting for Hannah to wake, a deep sense of uncertainty came over Maddie. She had spent so much time trying to support Hannah, to give her the space and safety she needed to figure things out, but now it seemed that the outside world was creeping in. The question was, how would Hannah react to it? Would she accept Lisa's help, or would she see this as another burden to carry?

But the really big question was, would it cause her to shut down again?

Footsteps on the stairs made them all look up, and a moment later, Hannah appeared at the top of the staircase, her hair tousled from sleep, her flannel pajamas rumpled. Her eyes were tired, but she smiled faintly when she saw Maddie and Schatzi.

"Morning," she murmured, rubbing her eyes as she made her way down.

Maddie stood, her heart pounding as she crossed the room to meet Hannah at the bottom of the stairs. "Morning, Hannah," she said. "We need to talk about something."

Hannah's brow furrowed, her gaze darting to the sofa where Lisa sat, still and tense. Her expression shifted instantly from confusion to recognition to fear. "What's she doing here?" she asked, her voice edged with annoyance.

Maddie placed a gentle hand on her arm. "Lisa's here to help, Hannah. That's it. She found out about the baby and wants to offer her support."

Hannah's face paled, and she took a step back, her eyes wide with panic. "I didn't tell anyone," she whispered. "I didn't want anyone to know."

Lisa stood up, her hands raised in a placating gesture. "I'm sorry, Hannah. I really am. I didn't mean to find out. I just overheard from someone in town, and when I figured it out, I couldn't just do nothing."

"Who's talking about this? It's my business." Hannah's eyes filled with tears, and she shook her head, her voice trembling. "Does Trevor know? I don't want him to. I don't want any of this."

Schatzi frowned. "Take a breath, Hannah. It's all going to be okay."

Maddie's heart ached as she watched the girl crumble before her. This was exactly what she'd been afraid of. "Hannah, I know this is upsetting and not what you were prepared for," she said. "But Lisa isn't here because she's against you. She's here to offer help, and you don't have to make any decisions right now."

Hannah wiped at her eyes, her body trembling as she looked from Maddie to Lisa. "I just...I can't do this. It's too much."

Maddie wrapped her arms around Hannah, pulling her into a hug as the girl's sobs wracked her body. The girl was so easily upset these days. Had to be the extra hormones in her system. Maddie could feel the weight of Hannah's fear, her overwhelming sense of helplessness, and it broke her heart.

"Hey, you're not doing this alone, remember?" Maddie whispered, her voice steady. "We're all here for you. One step at a time, okay?"

Hannah nodded against her shoulder, her sobs slowing as she took deep, shaky breaths. Maddie held her for a while before pulling back and looking her in the eye. Hannah was calming down a little.

"Let's talk to Lisa," Maddie said gently. "Let's hear what she has to say. And if you don't want to do anything with that information, you don't have to. You're in control. This is your life. Your decisions. Your baby, right?"

"Right." Still Hannah hesitated, her tear-filled eyes flicking to Lisa, who stood quietly by the fire. After a long pause, she nodded, her voice barely a whisper. "Okay."

"Good girl," Schatzi said.

Maddie gave her a small, encouraging smile, and together they moved toward the sofa, where Lisa sat down again, her eyes filled with a mix of concern and relief.

As the four of them sat down together, the fire crackling in the background, Maddie knew that the road ahead remained uncertain. But in this moment, at least, they were moving forward.

And for now, that had to be enough.

Chapter Sixteen

The rest of Christmas Day passed quietly, but not without some tension. After Hannah had agreed to sit down with Lisa, the two of them had spoken for over an hour while Maddie and Schatzi gave them space.

From the kitchen, Maddie could hear bits and pieces of the conversation: Lisa offering support; Hannah hesitantly sharing details about the pregnancy; once, there was some laughter, but voices had been raised too.

Maddie did her best to stay out of earshot. She knew how delicate the situation was, and that Hannah needed to feel in control of the conversation. Maddie did not want to do anything to jeopardize that.

When both girls finally emerged from the living room, they looked exhausted but lighter, as if a weight had been lifted. Lisa left soon after, with a promise to return and help in any way she could. The visit had been unexpected, and though it had shaken Hannah, Maddie could see that Lisa's kindness had begun to break through the layers of fear and uncertainty Hannah had been carrying. It was a start.

Maybe Lisa had even helped reinforce the feeling of

support Hannah had. Knowing she had someone else in her corner had to bring Hannah some peace, didn't it?

Maddie had called Becca, and they'd had a nice chat. When she'd finished, she'd encouraged Hannah to call her dad, who was working. Maddie knew he had to be missing his daughter on Christmas Day, regardless of everything that was going on.

Thankfully, Hannah had obliged Maddie and seemed happier for it.

Now, as the evening drew to a close and the glow of the Christmas tree lights reflected softly in the window, Maddie sat with Schatzi in the living room, both of them sipping tea. The fire crackled, its warmth wrapping around them like a blanket, and Ernie lay sprawled on the rug, his eyes half-closed.

"Hard day for that girl," Schatzi said quietly, her voice cutting through the comfortable silence. She glanced toward the kitchen, where Hannah was cleaning up after dinner, her contribution to the meal. "But I still say she's stronger than she realizes."

"I agree." As much as Maddie wished things were different for all of them, there just wasn't a way to make that wish come true. "She's been through so much already and survived it. Even so, it's not fair. She's too young to deal with all of this."

Schatzi leaned back in her chair, cradling her tea in her lap. "Life isn't fair, sweetheart. You know that as well as anyone. Maybe more so. But it's what we do with the unfairness that matters." The lines around her eyes crinkled, and she gave Maddie a knowing look. "You're doing good by her, you know. Giving her a safe place, helping her find her way, being a go-between for her and her dad. You've become her Christmas miracle, whether she realizes it or not."

Maddie smiled faintly, though there was still a tightness in her chest. "I just want to protect her. She's so young. She shouldn't have to deal with all this on her own."

Schatzi set her tea down on the table beside her and gave

Maddie a pointed look. "That's why you're here. And now she's got Lisa, too. And me, and Sam, *and* her dad. You know she's not alone, Maddie. And neither are you."

Maddie blinked, the unexpected tenderness in Schatzi's voice catching her off guard. "Me?" When had the conversation become about her?

Schatzi's eyes never wavered. "You've spent so much time worrying about everyone else—about Hannah, about me, about Becca—that I think you've forgotten to take care of yourself."

Maddie opened her mouth to respond but found herself at a loss for words. She hadn't thought about herself in that way for a long time. Ever since Jack had passed, her world had revolved around surviving each day, one moment at a time. Being here, she'd thrown herself into taking care of others because it was easier than facing her own grief.

It made her feel like she was doing something worthwhile instead of just grieving the loss of her husband. All that did was carve out a bigger hollow inside her. Helping others, at least temporarily, seemed to fill that hollow up.

Schatzi reached across the space and took Maddie's hand in hers, her grip gentle but firm. "It's okay to lean on people, Maddie. You don't have to carry it all by yourself."

Maddie's throat tightened, and she looked away, blinking back the sudden tears that had welled up in her eyes. She had spent so long trying to be strong, to hold it all together, but Schatzi's words had pierced through the walls she had built around her heart.

"I know. I do," Maddie whispered, her voice trembling. "It's just...it's hard."

Schatzi smiled, her eyes warm. "I know it is. But you're not alone, sweetheart. You've got me, you've got Sam...and you've got a whole town full of people who care about you. Let them in."

The mention of Sam brought a flutter to Maddie's chest, and she realized how much his steady presence had come to mean to her. He had been there every step of the way, always offering support without asking for anything in return. And though she hadn't admitted it to herself before, Maddie knew that her feelings for him were growing stronger.

That was a hard thing to come to terms with. No man other than Jack had ever had space in her heart. Even thinking about another man in the terms of romantic possibility sent a small wave of guilt through her.

Even so, she knew Jack would want her to be happy. Almost as if he'd sensed something was about to happen to him, he'd said as much right before his heart attack, telling her that he wanted her to remarry if her heart led her to do so. She hadn't been able to bear that conversation and so she'd shut it down, but not before he'd had his say.

She shook her head, more to herself than to Schatzi. It was a lot to think about. Especially on Christmas Day, when memories of her life with Jack were foremost in her mind.

Just then, the sound of soft footsteps caught their attention, and Maddie looked up to see Hannah standing in the doorway. "All done. Kitchen is clean." She offered a small smile as she walked over to the couch and sat down next to Maddie.

"Thank you for doing that," Maddie said softly, shifting to make room for her. "That was really nice of you."

"Just pulling my weight," Hannah replied, pulling her knees up to her chest. She glanced at Schatzi, then back at Maddie. "I'm sorry about earlier...with Lisa. I know I kind of freaked out."

Maddie shook her head. "You don't have to apologize, Hannah. It was a lot to take in. How are you feeling?"

Hannah sighed, resting her chin on her knees. "I don't know. I'm relieved, I guess. Lisa was really nice. She didn't push me or anything. I can tell she's excited about the baby. More than I am, I think. At least so far. But mostly she just offered to help. Even with bills and stuff. I didn't expect that."

Schatzi nodded thoughtfully. "That's the thing about family. Sometimes they surprise you."

Hannah smiled faintly, her eyes gleaming with the reflection of the fire. "Yeah. I guess so."

The three of them sat in silence, listening to the soft crackling of the flames. Ernie shifted, rolling over to show his furry belly and making them all smile. Maddie could see that Hannah was still processing everything that had happened, but she was glad the girl had taken another step toward opening up. It was a small victory, but it mattered.

After a while, Hannah broke the silence, her voice barely above a whisper. "I don't know what to do next, though. I still haven't figured anything out, really."

Maddie shifted closer to her, resting a hand on Hannah's arm. "You don't have to figure it all out right now. One step at a time, okay? You have time to decide what's best for you and the baby."

Hannah nodded slowly, her eyes glistening with unshed tears. "The thing is, I can't get past feeling like I've messed everything up. I know this isn't what my mom wanted for me. Definitely not my dad, either. If I'm being honest, it's not what *I* wanted."

Schatzi leaned forward, her voice gentle but firm. "You haven't messed anything up, Hannah. Life doesn't always go according to plan, but that doesn't mean it's ruined. It just means you've got to take a different path. And that's okay."

Hannah sniffled, wiping at her eyes. "I wish my mom were here. She'd know what to do."

Maddie's heart squeezed at the pain in Hannah's voice. She knew that feeling all too well. The longing for someone who wasn't there, the ache of loss that never truly went away.

She wrapped an arm around Hannah's shoulders, pulling her close.

"I know," Maddie whispered, her voice thick with emotion. "But we're here for you, and we'll figure this out together. You're not alone. You have to remember that."

Hannah rested her head on Maddie's shoulder, her body relaxing into the comfort of the embrace. For a long time, they sat there in silence, the warmth of the fire wrapping around them like a protective cocoon.

Maddie felt a deep sense of connection in that moment—a bond that went beyond words. She had been so focused on helping Hannah, on taking care of Schatzi, that she hadn't realized how much she needed this. The quiet, the companionship, the shared vulnerability. It wasn't just about helping others—it was about allowing herself to be helped, too.

Even if that was hard to do, she understood how necessary it was.

Later that night, after Hannah and Schatzi had both gone up to bed and the house had settled into its quiet rhythm, Maddie bundled up and went out onto the porch, sitting in one of the rocking chairs and looking out at the moonlit snow. The world was still and silent, the mountains black against the navy-blue sky, the stars twinkling. It was a peaceful kind of quiet, the kind that didn't feel lonely.

She heard footsteps coming up the path and turned to see Sam and Fargo approaching, the two of them outlined by the light from inside the house. Fargo bounded up onto the porch, nuzzling his face into Maddie's hands, asking for pets.

"Hi, Fargo." Maddie obliged him before looking at Sam. "What are you doing out?"

He shrugged. "Fargo needed to go out. This seemed like as good a direction as any to go in."

She nodded, thinking he'd come this way on purpose, regardless of his explanation.

"I was going to ask if you minded that we joined you, but Fargo's lack of manners seems to have beaten me to it," Sam said, his voice low and gentle.

Maddie smiled and tipped her head toward the empty seat. "I'd love the company."

Sam took the other rocking chair, sitting beside her as they both gazed out at the snow-covered landscape. For a while, neither of them spoke, content to share the quiet moment.

"I talked to Hannah's dad today. You did good, getting her to call him. Bill needed that," Sam said after a while, his tone subdued. "You're really something with her. She trusts you."

Maddie glanced at him, her soul pleased by the compliment. "I hope she does. I only have her best interests at heart. And I'm really just trying to give her what she needs."

Sam nodded, his gaze still on the moonlit snow. "You're doing more than that, Maddie. You're giving her a place she can feel at home."

Maddie felt a lump form in her throat, and she looked down, her hands nervously occupied with Fargo's fur. She wasn't used to praise, but it was especially sweet coming from someone like Sam, who always seemed to know the right thing to say.

"I couldn't have done it without you," Maddie admitted, her voice barely audible. "You've been there every step of the way."

Sam turned to face her, his eyes full of an emotion she couldn't quite name. "I'm always here, Maddie. In case you didn't know that."

Maddie swallowed, her heart racing as she met his gaze. There was something unspoken between them, something that had been growing for weeks but had remained just beneath the surface. And now, sitting there in the luminous glow of the stars, Maddie felt the weight of it pressing down on her.

"Sam," she began, her voice trembling slightly. "Sometimes, I think I don't know what I'd do without you."

He smiled, a gentle, understanding smile that sent warmth flooding through her. "You don't have to know. I'm always going to be here. You and Schatzi are not alone. There's no reason for you to be."

Maddie let herself believe it, maybe because she needed to. It was time to let go.

And as they sat there, side by side, looking out at the moonlit mountains, it sank into Maddie she didn't have to carry the weight of the world on her own anymore. There was no need. She could let so much of it go.

Because she had people to share it with. Family. Friends. And they were enough.

In fact, they were more than enough.

Chapter Seventeen

The days following Christmas and New Year's felt like a slow exhale, as though the tension that had been holding them all so tightly had started to loosen. The snow stopped falling, and the sky remained a pale, wintry blue, the crisp air carrying with it a sense of renewal.

Maddie had settled into a quiet routine, taking care of the house and Schatzi, checking in on Hannah, and finding moments to breathe amidst the daily tasks that were somehow lighter than they'd been before.

Hannah had begun to open up more after Lisa's visit. She was still scared at times, still uncertain, but Maddie could see that having someone connected to the baby's father in her life had eased some of her fears. The girl no longer carried the same heaviness around her, and though she still had a long road ahead, Maddie was relieved to see that she was beginning to accept help.

Not only that, she'd begun spending more time at her own home. Maddie hoped that meant Hannah and her dad were getting along better.

One afternoon, Maddie and Schatzi sat in the living room,

the smell of freshly baked bread wafting from the kitchen. The fire crackled softly, and the house felt unusually peaceful. Ernie had found a spot on Schatzi's lap, purring contentedly as Schatzi ran her hand absentmindedly through his fur.

"I think I'll go into town next week," Schatzi said, breaking the comfortable silence.

Maddie raised an eyebrow. "Into town? Are you sure? Your shoulder still needs time to heal. You might get jostled or—"

Schatzi waved a hand dismissively. "I've had plenty of rest and recovery already. I'm going stir-crazy in here, and I need to stretch my legs. Besides, I'm not made of glass, Maddie. A little outing will do me good. You're fine company, but I'd like to see how the rest of the world is doing."

Maddie smiled, though her head protested a little at Schatzi's stubbornness. She had grown used to having her aunt around the house, filling the space with her sharp wit and comforting presence. The idea of her going out and about again was a reminder that life was slowly moving forward, whether Maddie was ready for it or not.

"If you're sure," Maddie said, leaning back in her chair. "We could go into town together. Maybe grab lunch at the diner. That would be nice, wouldn't it?"

Schatzi's eyes twinkled with amusement. "Ah, so you're coming along to keep an eye on me. I see how it is."

Maddie laughed. "Is that so wrong? I just don't want you pushing yourself too hard."

Schatzi gave her a knowing smile, her expression soft. "You've got a good heart, Maddie. But you don't need to fuss over me. I'm a tough old broad."

Maddie nodded, though she couldn't help but feel protective of Schatzi. The thought of losing her aunt—the last real connection she and Becca had to their mom's family—was something she tried not to dwell on. Schatzi was strong, but

Maddie knew she wouldn't be around forever. The thought lingered in the back of her mind, even as she shoved it aside for now.

As they sat in comfortable silence, the sound of quick knock was followed by the front door opening. Maddie glanced toward the entryway and smiled as Sam stepped inside, his usual dusting of snow on his coat and boots. Fargo trotted in behind him, shaking off the snow with a happy woof of greeting.

Ernie lifted his head and looked as though he could have done without the interruption.

"Afternoon," Sam called out, his deep voice warm as he smiled at Maddie and Schatzi. "I come bearing firewood."

Maddie got up and walked over to him with a grateful smile. "You're not going to stop spoiling us, are you?"

Sam chuckled, setting the wood by the hearth. "Can't have you freezing in this weather. Besides, it gives Fargo an excuse to come by."

"So this is all Fargo's doing?"

"That's right."

Maddie's heart fluttered at the casual way he said it, and she couldn't help the warmth that spread through her. Over the past few weeks, Sam had become a constant in her life—a steady, calming presence that she hadn't realized she needed until it had arrived. She hadn't fully processed her feelings for him, mostly because she wasn't ready to, but the way he made her feel—the safety, the companionship—was undeniable.

"How's everything?" Sam asked, looking from Maddie to Schatzi.

Schatzi smiled, her hand stroking Ernie's back. "We're doing just fine, Sam. Though I'm getting restless being stuck in this house."

Sam's eyes twinkled with amusement. "I can imagine. How's the shoulder?"

"Better," Schatzi said with a nod. "I'm planning on going into town next week."

Sam raised an eyebrow. "You sure you're ready for that?"

Schatzi huffed. "I'm ready. Maddie doesn't think so, but I'm not letting this sling keep me down any longer than it has to."

Maddie laughed, shaking her head. "I'll make sure she takes it easy."

Sam smiled, his gaze lingering on Maddie before he turned to Schatzi. "Well, if you need any help, just let me know. I'll drive you into town, if you want."

Schatzi grinned. "Always the gentleman."

He sat and the three of them fell into easy conversation, the warmth of the fire and the glow of the afternoon sun filtering through the windows making everything feel calm and comforting.

Maddie realized how much she had come to enjoy these moments—small, quiet interactions that reminded her that life was moving forward in wonderful ways she hadn't expected. The house felt less like a place of refuge and more like a home, filled with warmth and connection.

Later that afternoon, Maddie decided to go for a walk before she started on dinner. The sun was beginning to set, glazing the snow-covered landscape with a pink and orange glow. The air was cold but crisp, and Maddie found herself breathing deeply, savoring the quiet of the mountains.

As she walked through the woods, the familiar crunch of snow under her boots, she thought about everything that had changed over the past few weeks. She had come to this mountain house expecting to hide away from the world, to avoid the pain of her grief. Instead, she had found something unexpected—a community, a purpose, and, most of all, a sense of healing that she hadn't thought possible.

She wasn't completely healed, of course. Grief wasn't

something that disappeared overnight. But the weight of it had lessened, and Maddie found herself looking forward to each new day in a way she hadn't for a long time.

It was a good feeling. One she hadn't been sure would ever return. Now that it had, she didn't want to lose it again.

The path through the woods led to a small clearing that had a fantastic view of the Smoky Mountains, and as Maddie reached it, she spotted Sam standing near the edge, looking out at the horizon. Fargo was by his side, sniffing at the ground, his tail wagging happily when he saw her.

Maddie smiled and walked toward him, her breath forming small clouds in the cold air. Sam turned when he heard her approach, an easy smile crossing his face.

"I didn't expect to find you out here," Maddie said, stopping beside him.

Sam nodded, his eyes on her now. "I needed to clear my head. This is my favorite spot to do that."

Maddie's gaze followed his to the distant mountains. "I can see why."

They stood in silence, watching as the last light of the day faded, leaving the sky a deep, dusky blue. The stars had begun to appear, twinkling faintly against the backdrop of the night, and the quiet of the woods wrapped around them like a blanket.

After a while, Sam spoke, his voice even and steady. "I've been thinking about what you said the other night. About not doing everything on your own."

Maddie glanced at him, her heart fluttering. She remembered their conversation on the porch, the intimacy of it, the way he had looked at her with such understanding.

"I meant it," she said quietly, her voice barely above a whisper. "I don't want to do it alone anymore."

Sam turned to face her, his eyes filled with something Maddie hadn't seen before, something that made her heart race. He took a step closer, his breath visible in the cold air, and reached out to gently take her hand.

"You don't have to," he said, his voice low and warm. "I've said it before, but I'll say it again. I'm here, Maddie. I've always been here."

Maddie's breath caught in her throat, her heart pounding in her chest as she met his gaze. There was a tenderness in his eyes, a gentle strength that made her feel safe—safer than she had felt in a long time. And in that instant, standing there in the quiet of the mountains, she realized that she wasn't afraid anymore.

She wasn't afraid to let someone in. Not when that someone was a man like Sam. Calm, caring, easy-going in a way that made her feel comfortable being herself.

Slowly, Maddie nodded, a smile tugging at the corners of her lips. "I know," she whispered.

Sam's smile widened, and he gently squeezed her hand, his touch warm against the cold. For a long moment, they stood there, the silence between them filled with unspoken words. It was a quiet, intimate connection. One that didn't need to be rushed or explained.

They had time.

And as the stars twinkled above them, Maddie knew that this was the beginning of something new. Something she hadn't been expecting but was ready to embrace.

She was done with just surviving. She wanted to live. To enjoy her life. It was good to look forward to what came next, but it was even better to have something wonderful to look forward to.

That made all the difference.

Chapter Eighteen

The last days of winter passed in a slow, gentle rhythm, and as the snow began to melt, Maddie felt the stirrings of something new blossoming inside her. The mountain house, once a place where she had come to escape her pain, had become her home—one filled with love, friendship, and the quiet strength of healing.

Her plans to only stay for Christmas were long gone. At some point, she'd have to return to her place, but it would only be temporary. Just to tie up loose ends and make whatever arrangements were necessary.

With Schatzi's blessing, which she'd already given, Maddie knew her future was here, in the mountains with her aunt. This was where she belonged.

Every day, the grief that had once felt so heavy now seemed lighter, and though it still lived inside her, it no longer defined her. In many ways, she felt reborn.

Hannah had settled into a routine that gave her a sense of stability. Lisa had kept her promise, visiting often to offer her support, and the bond between the two girls had deepened with each passing day. Hannah's relationship with her dad was improving, too.

There remained moments of fear, moments when Hannah would look lost and uncertain, but she wasn't facing them alone. She had a network of people who cared about her, who would walk with her through the challenges ahead, and she knew that.

Maddie had watched her grow, watched her transform from the frightened girl who had shown up at Schatzi's house week after week to someone who was beginning to find her voice. There was still uncertainty, of course, but Maddie knew Hannah was strong enough to face it. And that, more than anything, filled her heart with hope.

Schatzi, ever the matriarch of their little family, had made a full recovery from her fall. She grumbled about the cold and insisted she could handle things on her own, but Maddie could see the twinkle in her aunt's eyes whenever they all sat together by the fire, sharing stories and laughter.

The house had become a place of warmth and connection, and Schatzi reveled in the company. In fact, Maddie thought it had done both of them a world of good to have each other. One more reason to move here permanently.

The other big reason was Sam.

Sam had become more than just a neighbor. Over the months, their friendship had deepened into something more, something that neither of them had tried to label. It was an unspoken understanding, a quiet affection that had grown between them in the stillness of the mountains.

They hadn't rushed anything, hadn't forced anything. Instead, they had let the connection grow naturally, day by day, until it had become as steady and stable as the mountains around them.

As winter gave way to early spring, the snow began to

melt, revealing patches of green that promised the renewal of life.

Maddie stood on the porch one morning, the crisp air cool against her skin as she looked out at the horizon. The world felt new again, as if it were waking up after a long sleep, and Maddie couldn't help but feel the same way.

She was different now. Stronger. Lighter. More at peace. She knew who she was without Jack, too, and surprisingly, she liked that person. She was ready for the next chapter of her life, whatever that might be.

She started to go in but stopped as she heard the sound of footsteps behind her. Pleased, she turned to see Sam walking up the porch steps, the ever-faithful Fargo trotting beside him. He smiled when he saw her, the kind of smile that made the sun feel a little warmer.

"Good morning," Sam said, his voice low and familiar.

"Morning," Maddie replied, leaning against the porch railing. "Beautiful, isn't it?"

Sam stood beside her, looking out at the mountains. "It is. This time of year is something special. Feels like a new start."

Maddie nodded, the quiet truth of his words settling over her. A new start. That was exactly what it felt like.

For a few moments, they stood in comfortable silence, the early morning sun casting a soft glow over the landscape. Fargo sniffed at the ground nearby, his tail wagging lazily, and Maddie couldn't help but feel a deep sense of contentment.

"Have you thought about what you're going to do now? What comes next?" Sam asked after a while, his voice gentle.

Maddie looked at him, her heart swelling with gratitude for everything he had been to her over the past few months. "I have," she said. "And I think it's me staying. Here, I mean. With Schatzi."

And him.

Sam turned to face her fully, his hand brushing lightly against hers. He cleared his throat. "You're sure?"

Maddie smiled, the warmth of happiness spreading through her. "I'm sure. This place...it's home now. In so many ways. And I don't want to leave it behind."

Sam's smile widened, and he took her hand, his fingers lacing through hers. "I'm glad," he said quietly. "I like the idea of you staying."

Maddie's heart fluttered, and she leaned into him, resting her head on his shoulder as they looked out at the mountains together. For the first time in what felt like forever, the future didn't seem so uncertain. It didn't feel overwhelming or scary. It felt like something she could walk toward, step by step, with Sam by her side.

It felt like something she could genuinely look forward to.

Later that afternoon, they all gathered around the kitchen table—Schatzi, Hannah, Sam, and Maddie—for one of their regular meals together. Except this time, Lisa and Bill had joined them.

The house was filled with the smell of fresh bread, roast beef, and roasted vegetables, and the sound of laughter echoed through the rooms as Schatzi regaled them with stories of her younger days in the mountains.

Hannah sat between her dad and Lisa, the two girls exchanging knowing smiles as they listened to Schatzi's wild tales, and Maddie couldn't help but marvel at how far they had all come. The house felt alive with love and laughter, a stark contrast to the quiet isolation she had once sought.

As the meal came to an end, Schatzi raised her glass of lemonade, her eyes sparkling with mischief. "I'd like to propose a toast," she said, her voice filled with warmth.

Maddie raised her own glass, smiling at her aunt. "What are we toasting to?"

Schatzi grinned, her eyes dancing with affection as she

looked around the table. "To new beginnings," she said. "And to family, in all its messy, wonderful forms."

The room fell silent as everyone took in the weight of her words. Then, slowly, they all raised their glasses, smiles spreading across their faces.

"To new beginnings," they echoed.

As they clinked their glasses together, Maddie felt a swell of emotion rise within her. It wasn't just a toast. It was a declaration of everything they had been through, everything they had overcome. They had faced heartache, loss, and uncertainty, but they had come out the other side stronger, bound together by the love and friendship they had found in one another.

After dinner, Sam went out to take Fargo for a walk, and Maddie decided to join him. The two of them stepped out into the cool evening air, the sky painted in hues of pink and orange as the sun dipped behind the mountains.

As they walked along the familiar path through the woods, Maddie slipped her hand into Sam's, the connection between them solid and sure. They didn't need to speak. They had already said everything that needed to be said. Instead, they walked in comfortable silence, the sound of Fargo's paws and their own footsteps crunching in the leaves the only noise around them.

When they reached the clearing that had become their spot, the last light of the day fading into twilight, Maddie stopped and turned to face Sam. He looked down at her, his eyes filled with the same warmth that had been there since they'd met.

"Thank you," Maddie said softly, her voice filled with emotion. "For everything."

Sam smiled, reaching up to gently cup her cheek. "You don't need to thank me, Maddie. I'm just glad you're here. Glad that you've become a part of my life."

Maddie leaned into his touch, her heart swelling with love. She hadn't expected to find this. Hadn't expected to find *him*. But now, standing there in the quiet of the evening, she knew that this was exactly where she was meant to be.

"I love you," she whispered, the words slipping out before she could stop them, but she wasn't bothered by what she'd admitted. The words had come from her heart, and she meant them.

Sam's eyes softened, and he pulled her closer, pressing a gentle kiss to her forehead. "I love you too."

And in that moment, as they stood together beneath the first stars of the evening, Maddie knew that she had found her home.

Not just in the house or in the mountains—but in the people who had become her family. In the love that surrounded her.

In Sam.

She'd come to the mountain house to take care of her aunt, but Maddie knew she'd needed some taking care of, too. The loss of Jack would always be with her, but she knew he'd have liked Sam. He'd be happy that she was taking this next step. Happy that she'd found a place that had done so much for her. That had helped heal her.

With that kind of assurance in her heart, she moved closer to Sam. The mountains really had brought her back.

Back to life. Back to happiness. Back to love.

Looking for the latest Maggie Miller? Check out Hideaway Bay.

Want to know when Maggie's next book comes out? Then don't forget to sign up for her newsletter at her website!

Also, if you enjoyed the book, please recommend it to a friend. Even better yet, leave a review and let others know.

Completed Series by Maggie Miller

The Blackbird Beach series:

Gulf Coast Cottage

Gulf Coast Secrets

Gulf Coast Reunion

Gulf Coast Sunsets

Gulf Coast Moonlight

Gulf Coast Promises

Gulf Coast Wedding

Gulf Coast Christmas

The Compass Key series:

The Island

The Secret

The Dream

The Promise

The Escape

Christmas on the Island

The Wedding

About Maggie:

Maggie Miller thinks time off is time best spent at the beach, probably because the beach is her happy place. The sound of the waves is her favorite background music, and the sand between her toes is the best massage she can think of.

When she's not at the beach, she's writing or reading or cooking for her family. All of that stuff called life. She hopes her readers enjoy her books and welcomes them to drop her a line and let her know what they think!

Maggie Online:

www.maggiemillerauthor.com
www.facebook.com/MaggieMillerAuthor

Made in the USA
Las Vegas, NV
06 December 2024

13360413R10080